BETTER THAN YOUR EX

BOOK TWO IN THE CASSIDY AND CAHIR SERIES

JIMI GAILLARD-JEFFERSON

To your health. To your happiness.

GET TO KNOW GUY

Spend more time with the most beloved character in the New Money Girls universe- Guy. It was love at first sight when he saw O'Shea. She...felt a little different.

This is a FREE novel. The link is in the back of the book. Happy reading!

CHAPTER ONE

Cassidy

I stood in that elevator with Cahir and heard two words run in a loop in my mind over and over again.

Zion's pregnant.

Of course she was. Of course. Their great fated love couldn't end with something as simple as him walking away. Oh, no. It couldn't fall away and make way for his hand in mine. For walks in the farmer's market and eyes screwed shut while his mouth admitted a future with her was not the best possible option. It couldn't be nights that spread me wide and made me loose for him, wild for him. It couldn't be smiles and suspended breath in the morning until we each brushed our teeth. It couldn't be lunches cooked together or dinners where we laughed and laughed until we fell silent because it was just too good, too comfortable, too easy, too right. Too much like what the best kind of forever looked like.

It couldn't be secrets. The embarrassing ones. It couldn't be the bone deep knowledge that we could tell each other anything and it would be okay because there would be so much between us but there would never be judgment. It couldn't be private jets and hotel rooms that made you catch your breath and relax. It couldn't be finding that what we shared was the same no matter what city we took it to. It couldn't be a shared glance that had us both rushing back to the hotel and smiling when we failed and made it to a cabana instead.

It couldn't be understanding and trust and intimacy and openness. It couldn't be love and sex and friendship. It couldn't be honesty.

Zion was fucking pregnant.

There was a ringing in my ears. The silver of the elevator doors blurred but there were no tears. Thank the ancestors. I put my pride to the side for Cahir once. I for damn sure didn't want to do it again.

Fuck, Zion was pregnant.

I softened my knees. I focused on that. On using my meditation breathing. On unclenching my hands. On not grinding my teeth. On hearing something besides the high pitched sound in my ears.

The elevator opened and dry air whooshed into the space, over my face. The ringing dissipated. And I heard Cahir.

Had he been talking that entire time? What was there for him to say? Explanations, probably. Men always had something reasonable to say about their shitty behavior after they got caught. Reasons why it wasn't their fault. Reasons why you should keep fucking them. Keep smiling. Keep showing up. Hadn't Kevin taught me that?

Hadn't I learned? After everything, hadn't I learned to protect myself, to stay safe, to understand that sometimes fear had its place and should be followed?

Love. The great thing we were all supposed to chase.

The thing that was supposed to make life worth living. The thing that was supposed to elevate a woman and truly make her a member of society. Oh I knew how different it was for me at work when I said I had a boyfriend, when I dropped Cahir's name. I knew how much more my clients respected me, saw me as their equal. I knew how strangers viewed me when I showed up on Cahir's arm and- fuck it all.

I almost walked right up to his car. I almost went to the passenger door and waited for him to open it for me.

I laughed. The sound was shrill and enough to shut Cahir the fuck up. Praise.

"Cash-"

"Shut up." I was proud of how steady my voice was. How it carried even though it was so deep. "Shut up, Cahir. You've said enough-gotten me to say enough today, haven't you?"

Color bloomed over his cheeks. His eyes stopped boring into mine and focused instead on his shoes.

"I'm going home. You aren't going to follow." I heard the breath shudder out of him. It would have meant something, his hurt, even ten minutes ago. But I was sure that the part of me that wanted to protect him was dead. "And since space seemed to be exactly what you needed to help you embark on this new chapter in your life-"

I couldn't help it. I laughed again. It sounded more hysterical than the first laugh. I cut it short because there was something besides laughter building in my chest.

"Stay the fuck away from me. When I'm ready to talk to you again, see you again, if I ever am, I'll call you. Don't-" I threw open my car door and flung myself inside. "Stay away from me."

I peeled out of the lot. He didn't move. And when I looked into my rearview mirror his eyes were right there to meet mine.

CHAPTER TWO

Cassidy

"I'm not gonna say you're wrong." Junie walked into my office with a bounce in her step that I didn't understand until I looked down.

"Cute shoes."

"They are. I didn't know you guys would have anything in the showroom in my size."

I didn't mean to but for the first time since the elevator I laughed. A misused, broken sound. One that spoke of rust, disuse. Neglect.

I scoffed. "It's only been twenty-four hours."

"Twenty-seven." Junie slid her phone back into her back pocket and sank down into the couch.

The boots she wore were cute. That's why I bought a pair for her. I wasn't surprised that she found them. Only that it took so long and that the long skirt with its higher slit paired so well with them. If Junie weren't my best friend I would have been jealous. I could never make a torn NWA concert tee look that good.

"Twenty-seven?"

"Yeah. You texted me 'fuck men' exactly twenty-seven hours ago."

"And you didn't back me up." I sat down next to her and sighed. "It's been twenty-seven hours, and I am miserable."

"So go back to him."

My mouth might have fallen open. "Just-You think I should just go back."

"If you're happier with him." Junie shrugged. "I don't even know why you left him though. So maybe if you tell me a little bit more of your business I'll be better equipped to say what you want to hear."

I laughed again. And I told her.

"Fucking shit. What in the goddamn fuck? Are you fucking kidding me? He did the fuck what?"

I nodded. "Yes. All of that."

"Can I tell you the part that pisses me off the most?"

"God, yes." I rubbed my hands together. "Finally."

"That he knew. He knew and then thought getting you to say you loved him would somehow make it all magically okay."

"Yes!" I jumped to my feet. "You're an absolute coward in your office. Can't even look me in the eye. But you can fuck me in an elevator until I say what you want to hear. Then you drop the bomb on me. Why manipulate me like that? Why not just tell me? Why not just-"

"Be honest. Be open," Junie said.

"Why not just be my friend?"

Junie's hand slipped into mine. "I'm sorry, Cass."

I didn't know what she was apologizing for. The loss of trust in my relationship? The loss of a friendship? My sorrow? The corners of me that held a shame that didn't belong to me?

I sat down again. "I don't know what to do."

"Do you really love him?"

I nodded.

"Huh." She laughed.

"What?"

"Wasn't supposed to be you, I guess." She rubbed her shoulder. "I might have to rethink some things."

"Like what?"

She shook her head. "This isn't about me. This is about you. What you need?"

I should have pressed her. I should have made her admit to me what was wrong, what was going on. But I was so relieved that there was a place, a person, that could focus on just me that I let it go.

"I wish I could let him go." I took a deep breath. "I wish I could just run from it, from all of it."

"You could," Junie said. "But what's the fun in running if you don't have all the facts?"

∞

Cahir

I felt the absence of her. And they weren't anything alike, but I found myself comparing what it was to lose Zion to what it was to lose Cash. It took me a day to realize there was no comparison. The loss of Zion was about confusion. What did I do? Did I do anything? How could she be here one day and gone the next? Did she miss me? Did she think of me? Did she do anything at all?

Had I imagined her? The way her body felt? The way mine felt when I was connected to her in any way? Had I imagined her skin and the eternity in her eyes? The softness of her voice and the rigidity of her spine? The way every-thing seemed like it just wasn't quite good enough for her?

Confusion. Then desperation because I needed to know. I needed to know that I'd felt something. That she felt it too. I needed to know that she wasn't fabricated in my mind.

Losing Cash-

Cash was the other side of the coin. The cool side of the pillow. She was realer than me. More vivid than me. More alive. I injected her into my veins and used what she gave me to get through my day, to plan for and move toward the future. I knew her laugh lines and the creases that formed between her eyes when she was angry. I knew the arch of her eyebrows and her back. I knew the quiet of her foot-steps and the grace in her hands. I knew the laughter that lived in her eyes. I knew her curls. I knew each strand of her hair personally. Intimate friendships I wanted to hold onto for the rest of my life.

I knew her sleep and how she moved when pleasant dreams overtook her. I knew what she smelled like after a long day of work. I knew what her mouth tasted like when sleep still coated it. I knew how often she cleaned and the order she did it in.

I knew why she left.

Hadn't I expected it? Wasn't that why my mouth went dry and my mind blank the day she came to my office? A week. That was only a week ago. I knew why I didn't have her voice. I knew why I didn't have her hands in mine, on me. I knew. I should have prepared for it. I should have known. Didn't Zion say there would only ever be me and her?

In the week without Cash I held my phone in my hand and considered it. I considered calling Zion, hearing her

out. Maybe there was something different. Maybe there was something new. Maybe she found the perspective that would make it all okay. Maybe she found a reason that wouldn't make me wonder if it would be easier to leave life behind.

I thought about what it would be like if I went back to her. If she got what she wanted and I was by her side while she had the child. The answer was fast. Winning was its own kind of approval. Winning was encouragement to do it again, do more. Winning was all she would need to continue down the path we were already on. All the proof she needed to know that my life, my wants, my needs, my thoughts, were forever second to hers.

I didn't call Zion.

I didn't call Cash either. I saw it on her in the parking garage. I saw how close to breaking she was. I saw how easy, in her anger, it would be for her to end us. I stayed silent.

Then my phone rang. A time. A place. And then silence again.

I wore a suit to the coffee shop she picked. The one I hated because it was full of doctors and college students and light. Just a room full of people high on what they would be one day and the things they did that day. Conversation after conversation about the banal and the ridiculous.

I ordered green tea for Cash. Thought about coffee but it felt like everything in my body was in a rush. What would I do with caffeine? I sat at a table by one of too many windows in that goddamned place and waited for Cash.

When I saw her walk up the sidewalk, heavy, oversized purse on her shoulder, I thought I'd been shot. Just the sight of her. Long, small, delicate. Dangerous. The woman that made me believe in fairies and witches. I hated her car. It wasn't good enough for her. I didn't know why she drove it. I hated her purse. Lumpy thing. Why didn't she own a Birkin? I would buy her a Birkin. A dozen of them. And a car. A Range Rover. Better than mine. Or maybe I would get her a driver.

I stood. I didn't expect her to touch me. Shit, I didn't expect her to look at me. But she did. She hugged me. The kind of hugs I'd come to expect from her. The ones that pressed her whole body against mine and lasted until our heart beats were in sync. Until my heart beat was in sync with hers. I wasn't fool enough to believe I was in charge.

"You look beautiful," I said.

She did. A sweater hung off her shoulder and her pants clung to her hips, to her, like a second skin. Big jewelry and lipstick that made me wish we were what we used to be. Made me wish it was okay to lean in close. Hair that smelled like home and tickled my face in all the places it used to.

"Thank you." She sat. "Thanks for the tea."

I nodded and sat down too.

"Nice suit."

A smile flirted with her lips but I ignored the hope I felt.

"Thanks," I said. "My stylist is the shit."

"Yeah." She took a sip of her tea. "Tell me what happened."

"Zion's six months pregnant."

Because it was Cash it was different. I didn't have to wait for understanding to come. Her hands went to the scars on mine.

"I'm so sorry." Her fingers were gentle. Maybe I didn't look as strong as I thought I did. "I'm so sorry."

I told my parents in the week Cash was gone. Once the shock wore off their faces they congratulated me. My mother hugged me. My father pressed beer and a cigar into my hands. So I had to smile. With everyone I told, I had to smile. It felt as wrong as what happened to me.

I nodded and breathed. Looked down at Cash's hands, studied the lines of skin that made abstract patterns over her knuckles. Told myself I wasn't going to cry in a room full of people so bland and unoriginal that they probably all hid their cocaine in the same place.

"Is that why she-"

"O'Shea thinks it's because she started showing. That's why she left me alone."

Cash shook her head.

"It was O'Shea that told me. And she had a recording. Of Zion. Admitting to the whole thing. She told them over fucking mimosas and fruit how she planned out the whole thing. Ovulation tracker. Trip to the drug store to buy every condom in the place. How she didn't get the size of the holes in the condom right the first time."

Cash's hands balled into fists.

"Because she used a safety pin. Too big. She used a sewing needle. That worked better."

"Cahir."

"You're the only person I haven't had to pretend with. You've always been that person."

"I'm sorry."

"I'm sorry." I would have touched her. I would have grasped her hand in mine if I weren't such a coward. If I weren't so close to breaking my goddamned self. "I'm sorry that I disappeared. I'm sorry I didn't tell you as soon as I knew."

"That's what you're sorry for?"

I was good at tests. Good at avoiding traps and minefields. I was good at reading Cash.

I nodded. "Yes. I'm so sorry. I'll never stop being sorry. We're-I'm better than that."

"Okay." The sadness on her face was new to me. Panic inducing.

Her hands slid off the table and into her lap. But her eyes never wavered. Not once. Cinnamon brown and steady on mine.

"Our relationship, me as your girlfriend, that's over."

CHAPTER THREE

Cassidy

Leaving Cahir wasn't like leaving Kevin. Kevin was smooth. Smoother than smooth. He was oily. He touched you and left something behind that you were never quite sure you liked. You just said you did because it was him. And the rest of your life was a shit storm so why not a little something more?

Leaving Cahir-I left a piece of me at that table. His prints were all over that piece of me. So many that I couldn't see myself beyond them, couldn't remember what it had been before. And it called to me. Cried for me. Pushed me to silence one moment and screaming tears the next. It made me lose focus mid-conversation. Sharp looks from Gran. Sympathetic ones from Junie.

Junie still dragged me out for drinks every day after work. She wouldn't let me drink more than two.

"Fuck that. You don't need alcohol to heal yourself," she said.

And I loved her for that. Fiercely. Loved how she

guarded me and gave me a reason not to pour three fingers of vodka into my juice in the morning or break open a bottle of wine when I got home from work.

She signed me up for yoga and refused to join me. And she talked. Talked and talked until I came back in my skin and could talk back.

Except for one day. And I didn't say anything at first. What would I say? Speak and distract me from my own thoughts? Do for me what I can't do for myself? Help me, I'm crazy, I smell him, I hear his voice, feel his touch?

Even in that moment when we sat in the hole in the wall bar with its shitty wine selection and heaven sent cheesesteaks. One sat between Junie and I. Our second one. She winked when she ordered it. I might have laughed. I couldn't remember.

I couldn't focus on anything but what Cahir would feel like if he were there. The feel of his hand on the small of my back. His sigh of happiness. His other hand wrapped around the cheesesteak, confident as it made its way to his mouth. His thanks. I knew what he would say.

"Thank God. How'd you know I needed this, Cash?"

I blinked. It was real. Too real. And I was dizzy. Was I so deep in my mind that I could see and hear what I wanted most so vividly? No. No. It had to be-

I turned in my seat and he was there. He took a bite of my cheesesteak and winked at me. Dropped a kiss on Junie's forehead and laughed when she threatened him with bodily harm if he got steak juice or grease or ketchup or whatever on her forehead.

Then he sat next to me.

He smelled like...I thought I woke from a long sleep. A perfect sleep that almost went on too long. I almost smiled at him. Leaned into him. Kissed him.

I almost cried.

He saw it. His smile didn't soften because he felt some kind of victory. It wasn't pity either. We were wired to give each other what we needed most.

"What are you doing here?" I was proud of myself. My voice was natural. Even.

"Eating cheesesteaks. We're ordering another one right?"

"Abso-fucking-loutely," Junie said.

"And beer. This needs shitty beer." He ordered some. A pitcher of it.

"Why are you here?" My voice was a little tighter.

"You're not my girlfriend. Okay. I get it. I accept it. That that's over. You never said you weren't my friend. My best one."

I hadn't. Trust him to find the loophole. If I weren't an amalgamation of broken shards and jagged pieces, I would have smiled, teased him.

I couldn't tease him though. I couldn't feel anything but relief that there was a way to have him without having him. A way to keep him close without feeling like I'd given up something that I couldn't get back.

"We're still friends, Cash. Best friends."

There was too much insistence. An edge of desperation.

I slid the rest of the cheesesteak over to him and ordered us another one.

∞

Cahir

It was a risk to show up to drinks. But I didn't know what else to do. I didn't know how to live without her.

Ridiculous. I said I would never feel like that about a woman again. I said once was enough and I would protect myself. But it was different. I knew who I was when Cash was around and when she wasn't. I was still my own person.

There was the sense that I dropped something though. Something I needed. Something that would be a bitch to replace. Like keys or a wallet.

I couldn't spend the rest of my life, shit, I couldn't spend a week without her. So I said fuck it. I called Junie and believed her when she said she was only telling me where she and Cash were because she hoped Cash would fight, she hoped she would have a justifiable reason to swing on me.

I thanked her. Genuinely. And told myself it would be unfair to Melody if I threw up in the trash can in my office.

Cash looked like heaven and sitting beside her was my own personal kind of hell. Touch wasn't the same. Eye contact wasn't the same. Body language wasn't the same.

I knew, but hadn't ever taken the time to really appreci- ate, how easy we were. No thought or preparation. Like walking out of your house with no jacket, no umbrella, and no clue what the weather was going to be. You just knew it would be fine.

I tried. For the first time with Cash, I tried. And I knew I failed. Knew there was something I was missing. Some moment, some thing, some-fuck if I knew. But she did. And Junie did.

So I told Cash I was taking her to the farmer's market.

She held my hand when I reached for it. She laughed. And still there was something.

Couldn't put my finger on it. Too much of a coward to ask.

CHAPTER FOUR

Cassidy

The farmer's market was...interesting. Funny. I didn't know it would be so much fun to watch Cahir squirm. I didn't know it would make me so angry to watch an otherwise intelligent man refuse to understand. How could he not know what he'd done?

How could I be so stupid?

I let him back in. I woke up fully dressed with him in my bed. I watched movies with him. I couldn't cook with him but what kind of fucking line in the sand was that? He just told me where to meet him for lunch. Eventually he asked me about dinner.

And because I couldn't carve out the part of myself that I saved for him, I agreed. I put on a fucking dress. I touched up my makeup. I slid on heels and fluffed up my hair until it looked the way he liked.

I held his hand when we walked into the restaurant. When we were led to a dark corner with a small table that reminded me of another table in another dark restaurant in Miami. No one paid me any attention in Miami when Cahir made me come between courses. They didn't notice when I slipped under the table and proved that I was a little better at keeping quiet when I came than he was.

Too much. I didn't know memories could hit that way, hurt that way. I didn't know they could break in the part of me that I thought was safe from onslaught, the part of me that could just be a friend and forget I was once a lover.

"No."

It wasn't my voice that stopped him. It was that I pulled my hand out of his.

"No?"

"I don't want to sit there," I said.

He looked at the table. Back at me.

There had to be a safe place. There had to be a way that I could do this and not feel like a coward. Not that that mattered. "The bar. Can we sit at the bar?"

He shrugged. It wasn't until we were close enough to the bar that was as intimate and dark as the rest of the restaurant that he laughed. A full belly laugh. The kind that ended other people's conversations as they tried to figure out if they missed a good joke.

"Miami? Is that it?"

I hated him. Hated the way he knew me. "Sit down, Cahir. Let's have a nice, friendly dinner."

"Oh, we will." He held out my chair for me and before he sat, he ordered us drinks.

He knew what I wanted even though I hadn't told him.

I ran my fingers along the edge of the coupe glass that held my aviation and listened to him laugh again. I hated when he laughed when I was upset with him. It guaranteed that I wouldn't be able to hang onto my anger for more than a few minutes.

"I thought that dinner had me strung out," he said. "You can't sit at tables with me anymore?"

It should have been ridiculous to me too. I should have been able to laugh with him. To make light of it. To remind him how his ankles rolled and his calves knotted with Charlie horses when I made him come. But I couldn't. I couldn't.

I'd had him. Probed beyond friendship and saw the places he didn't even know he had. I gave him pieces of me and he made a home in them. He was gentle with me. I couldn't remember the last time I had a man that could be rough and gentle with me.

That was gone, and I hadn't cried about it. I tried to in the privacy of my own home. I tried to in Gran's shop with her arms around me. I tried and I tried but the tears didn't come until that night at the bar with the memory of him, the taste of him, the rightness of what we should have been, blazoned on my mind.

My chair was loud when he dragged it over the floor and closed the space between us. "I'm sorry, Cash. I'm so sorry."

I knew what he was apologizing for. And it wasn't enough. It wouldn't be enough. I would have to fix it on my own.

"It's okay." I dabbed under my eyes and prayed I didn't look as crazy as I felt. "I'll fix it soon. Real soon."

CHAPTER FIVE

Cassidy

The day was done. Delia was gone. Everyone was gone. Even Nadia. But the music was still loud as it poured out of my speakers. A newly opened bottle of wine sweat on the coffee table. The industrial sized fan whirred and the lights were bright every time the camera shuttered.

"What are you doing?" Junie bounded into the room with a bag that smelled like Chinese food. "I thought you took all your pictures for social media already."

"I did." I looked into the camera again. Striking the right balance of friendly, open, sexy, and not here for the bullshit wasn't easy and I wasn't sure I'd accomplished it.

"Listen." The bag made a dull sound when Junie dropped it on the coffee table. "I'm not feeding you if you can't give me straight answers."

"Is it Chinese?"

"Yeah. I picked some up for the bosses's monthly strategy meeting and got some for us."

I nodded. Delia had been printing off a lot of charts that day. I should have realized what that meant. "Dating. I'm going to start dating."

"On the internet?" Junie's face scrunched as if I'd just squatted and taken a shit in front of her. "How ghetto."

I laughed so hard I lost control of my body and pressed the shutter button on the bluetooth remote for my camera over and over again.

Junie scrolled through them once I got hold of myself again. "They aren't bad."

High praise from her. My work was done. I unpacked the Chinese food and handed Junie chopsticks. We got comfortable on the couch.

"So explain this to me."

I slurped up some shrimp lo-mein. "What's there to explain?"

"Why are you dating?"

"Because I'm single."

"You were single after Kevin."

"Touché, bitch."

She grinned. I wasn't dumb enough to think that saying something clever would distract Junie from the fact that I didn't answer her.

I sighed. "I can't sit in my apartment or at work all day thinking about what I lost. I can't-"

"I get it."

"Thank God. I don't."

Junie laughed and ate some of my lo-mein. "Kevin versus Cahir. Not really much of a battle is it?"

"Fuck."

"But the internet?"

"What is wrong with the internet?"

"Nothing. There's nothing inherently wrong with low-hanging fruit either."

"Bitch."

"I'm just saying. Look around. Guy. Cahir. Fine. Colton. None of them have dating profiles."

"Isn't that proving my point? At least in Cahir's case?"

"Is it?"

I hated Cahir. I hated Junie too. "A man with sudden baby mama drama?"

"You think that's not on these dating websites?" She rolled her eyes. "You think Cahir brought you sudden baby mama drama?"

"Secret baby?"

"Have you been buying ebooks again?"

"I don't have a boyfriend anymore."

"Fair."

I ate a dumpling and handed the box to Junie. I loved dumplings. Loved that no matter how shitty a Chinese restaurant was I could always count on the dumplings to taste the same.

"So you get on a trash ass dating site. You find a man with maybe a little coin-"

"-he has to have more than a little." I sighed in pleasure when I found the orange chicken.

"Again I say: Guy, Fine, Cahir, Colton. Do they use the interwebs to find love?"

"They're a small sample size."

"You're really not good at being wrong."

I laughed. "So what am I supposed to do?"

"What I do."

"Oh." I turned to face her. I forgot that Junie had a separate phone just to collect men's phone numbers. She had so many of them on rotation at any given time it was, she said, the only way to keep her life organized. "But what if I don't want to go outside?"

"Can't be wrong. And you're lazy. Wow." Junie tsked

and shook her head. "Fine. Try it your way. Live in the ghetto."

I smiled big. "It's going to be great. You'll see."

∞

Cahir

I saw Zion everywhere after I left her. I thought she put a homing device on me. Bugged my phone. Hired someone to follow me. The City was too big for me to see her as often as I did, to anticipate the sight of her every time I turned a corner.

I didn't think about what things would be like when Cash broke up with me. I didn't think about seeing her out and about without me. Why would I? We were always together. And when we weren't we were texting or talking about where we were.

When I walked into the trendy French restaurant blasting music that could have been curated by no one but O'Shea, I missed a step and almost tripped in my shock. A riot of red brown curls. I couldn't see her face but I didn't need to. I knew it was Cash. I just didn't know who the hell she was sitting across from.

He was buttoned up. Wore a suit like mine. But not. She taught me what custom looked like, what care looked like, what luxury and a good tailor made a person look like. He didn't have that. Probably got his hair cut at the mall. Probably read the menu online ahead of time and picked out the dishes she wasn't allowed to order because he wouldn't be paid for another few days. Couldn't see them but I was willing to bet all the money I had on me (which was probably more than he made in a month) that his shoes were scuffed. Cash hated people that couldn't be bothered to pay attention to their shoes.

Changed my mind. I wasn't going to the bar. I pointed to the table I was going to sit at, pretended I didn't see the host roll his eyes. Ignored his smile when I palmed him a fifty for my audacity. I was too focused.

I was perpendicular to their table. Cash looked like solid gold. He looked like a Cub Scout. When did she start liking men with cheeks that chubby? Was it a Winnie the Pooh fetish? She used to run her fingers along my cheekbones and tell me it wasn't fair. She asked me once if she could do something gross. When I was done laughing at her question, at the fact that she didn't know she could do anything to me, anytime, she licked them-my cheeks. When her tongue was back in her mouth, when she laughed, I showed her what gross really was. I swallowed her laughter, her screams, her sighs, her body.

"What are they drinking?" I pointed at Cassidy and the Cub Scout.

The server looked over at their table. "Umm...he has the house red. I think he asked the bartender to make something up for her."

"She hates it," I said. The server laughed but I was right. Cassidy could drink like a fish if you gave her a cocktail she liked. My father said she drank like an Irishman and asked why I didn't bring her around more.

And house red. Of course he was drinking the house red.

I scanned the drink menu and grinned when I found the drink Cash should have. "Send her this. Send Chubby Cheeks one too. And tell them their meal is on me. No, cancel their meal. Send them this."

I pointed to the menu items Cash deserved and probably hadn't ordered.

The server smiled. "What's your name? I mean, who should I say it's from?"

I grinned for the first time since I walked in and saw the love of my-Cash-Cassidy-sitting with another man. "She knows my name."

"I like you," the server said.

"I like you too."

"Now what do you want to drink?"

"A whiskey." I held my fingers close together then widened them. "And a whiskey. Impress me with your choice."

I got my drink at the same time Cash and the Cub Scout got theirs. Realized I wasn't lying when I said I liked the server. She blocked me from their view until she announced who sent their drinks, then stepped away with a sweep of her arm. Dramatics. I liked dramatics.

I loved Cash's face. The emotions that played across it. Some fast, the ones she needed to hide, others slow. The anger. The anger bloomed the slowest.

An angry Cash used to terrify me. I couldn't reach through the anger when she was angry. I couldn't touch her no matter how many times I ran my hands or my lips over her. But this...I loved it. Loved it because I saw what came first: longing. It passed over her face the fastest, but I recognized it. I felt it.

I accepted the anger the way I used to accept her kisses-with gratitude. With a bit of amazement that it was for me.

She enjoyed her dinner in spite of herself. Each bite a fight. A testament to the strength of her pride. And her focus...He tried. I had to give the Cub Scout that. He really tried. She dropped the line of the conversation so many times but he was right there to pick it back up, to try again. There to try to make her laugh again, to make her smile at him. But she forgot to laugh when she should. She didn't smile. Or when she did it was a forced, gruesome thing.

Because her attention was on me. Oh, her little looks were quick. The twitches of her hand as she reached for her purse, her phone, were subtle. The way she enjoyed the cocktail I picked for her, the one with 24 karat gold flakes in it, was muted. But I saw it all.

And I knew. I knew she was still mine.

CHAPTER SIX

Cassidy

It was my eighth first date. No. My tenth? Twelfth?

It was easy enough in the beginning. I created my profile and had a full inbox within forty-eight hours. I eliminated and blocked the worst of them: the ones that sent dick pics or asked where I lived and if I was up for some company. That was at least half of them. Then I deleted the ones that obviously couldn't afford me or carry on a decent conversation with me. The ones that looked like they only had one flat pillow on their bed and didn't wash their sheets. Or looked like they did have pillows and sheets but only because they lived with Mommy and Mommy wanted her little boy to have the best.

I got rid of the ones with kids. The ones that were bitter in their profiles. You know the ones. They had more to say about how they were tired of women wasting their time and being this or that than they did about themselves. Those men never showed up with anything of value. I got rid of the men that were too short.

I forced myself to smile about what was left and responded to their messages. Deleted the ones that thought they could talk to me for days and days without setting up a date. Blocked the ones that got aggressive or whiny when I didn't answer their messages in under five minutes.

I went on dates. And thought about Cahir every second. Compared Cahir to them. I couldn't help myself.

Cahir was funnier. In a dry kind of way. In a way that didn't throw anyone but him under the bus. It was exhausting to watch men laugh at their own misogyny, homophobia, transphobia, racism, and prejudice. To have to explain why I was leaving before we had our first course.

Cahir was more attentive. His eyes and attention stayed on me. They didn't track the other women in the restaurant. They didn't focus on some point beyond me. They weren't on his phone.

Cahir had class. And style. Even when he wore the things I didn't pick out for him. He didn't need to make a production of checking the time to make sure I saw his watch. He didn't need to push his jacket behind him like he was a matador with a cape to make sure I saw the lining. Or smooth his tie so I noticed its quality.

Cahir didn't need to brag about his wealth. It was hard won but it wasn't the core of who he was. I didn't need to see his American Express or the keys to his car. I didn't need to hear about all the things he had or did. He just saw to me, made sure that I knew I could have whatever I wanted. Made sure I knew that I didn't have to ask, there was no budget.

"Get what you want, Cash."

"Touch your wallet and die, Cash."

"Why are you spending your money when you could spend mine, Cash?"

Cahir made me comfortable. I knew I didn't have to

pretend. I could be myself. And I didn't have to give more than I was ready to. My presence was enough. My personality as it was impressed him. Every word that came out of my mouth was fascinating. He could and would talk to me, just talk, all night. And he heard me. He wasn't just waiting for me to be quiet so he could say the thing he thought was so clever.

Cahir wanted to know me. He didn't want to figure out what he needed to say to get in my pants.

Cahir had a raw but easy sexuality that draped casually over his shoulders and colored everything he did. It promised me pleasure but didn't press for it. He was not more or less of a man if I didn't take off my clothes for him. It would not make or break his self esteem. But if I did decide to take off my clothes...

Cahir was smarter. And he wasn't an asshole about it. He knew that he knew a lot. And he recognized that the more he learned the more he realized he didn't know. He probed for information, to expand his thinking and understanding. And he shared what he knew in a way that made you interested in what he had to say. He never wanted to make you feel dumb or less than.

The list went on. On and on. No matter how I looked at it-He was just better. And I thought I could live with that. I didn't expect to find him and then another man as great as him immediately. I knew it would take time. I knew I would be discouraged and disappointed.

And then I saw him.

There was a chance that I would have liked the man I was having dinner with. I couldn't remember his name, but there was a chance that I would have. There was a chance that he would make me laugh. He had once. There was a chance that he would have said something fascinating. There was a chance that I could order my own cocktail and actually like it. There was a chance that the next time we went out for dinner I wouldn't have to gently tell him that the dinner he ordered me didn't suit my tastes.

But that chance was gone. Evaporated like rain drops in the sun the moment Cahir sent over the perfect drink for me, made sure I got the perfect dinner. Dressed in a suit I picked out for him. One that used to live in my closet. One that I'd taken off him moments after he put it on. That was the first time he fucked me in my closet. The first time I realized that I was borderline obsessed with the way he touched me.

Faced with the reality of him, his physical presence in my space while I sat across from someone else, I was forced to admit there would never be anyone quite like him. And it pissed me off.

How dare he? After what he'd done? How dare he take away the sting of it with this longing for him?

My hands shook through dinner until I decided that there was only one thing to do. I had to wipe that smug little smile off his face.

CHAPTER SEVEN

Cassidy

I smiled when I drove to his house. Maybe I should have felt bad about that, about the anticipation that moved through me. Fuck that. I didn't have room for guilt or trepidation. For the first time in a long time I was going to have some fun. My kind of fun.

I checked my lipstick in my rearview mirror. Put on another coat. I fluffed up my hair until it was the way he liked, the way that always made him reach for me, grab me, throw me against something before his hands came around my waist and I went flying up a wall and fell down onto his-

My heels were loud on the concrete as I walked through his parking garage, away from my car, safe in the parking spot he got for me. The one he still paid for. I used the key fob he hadn't taken away. The key on the rose quartz keychain I still treasured. Still set in my window every full moon. The keychain that held his keys and mine.

And felt my anger ratchet up a few notches when I saw that there were two wine glasses on his counter and a bottle

of wine- a Sauterne and cognac blend that I found for him-
on ice. Open and waiting.

He was on the couch. Back to me. Eyes on the view
maybe. Or on the candles that burned all over his apartment. Everywhere but near his bed. There was no light
there.

He'd taken off his jacket and tie. They were laid over
the back of his couch. Tossed there. The way he'd tossed
them that day on the Lonely Third when he told me to
touch myself and tell him how it would be.

I went hot. So hot my vision blurred. I slammed the
door behind me.

He didn't move. Didn't flinch. There was just a "hello,
Cash," because he expected me and wanted me to know it.
Wanted me to know the candles and the wine weren't for
anyone else.

I kicked off my heels and put my purse in the place that
I always put my purse. It only made my body hotter, made
the pounding in my head louder, that that place was still
available. That there was a place for my shoes.

"You're a piece of shit," I said.

And he laughed. Just a little. Low and quiet and slow.
Like he wanted to savor my words. "Am I?"

"Worse than shit, you asshole."

"Come sit down. Tell me my sins."

Fuck him and his voice. "You don't tell me what to do."

"You've made that clear."

"And yet there you were tonight."

"It's not like you told me where you were having
dinner."

"As if that matters!"

"No. Of course it doesn't."

"Don't placate me like I'm some kind of child."

He hadn't turned to face me. He didn't have to. I knew

he could see my reflection in that wall of windows. Even if he couldn't he knew me well enough-

"The drink? Dinner? What kind of fucking point were you trying to prove? Were you trying to humiliate my date?"

"I wouldn't be able to do that if he was what you wanted, made sure you had what you wanted. Did he do that, Cash?"

I would throw the bottle of wine at him. I would rip his throat out. Then he wouldn't be able to send his voice to wrap around me, to constrict me like a fucking snake. "You don't get to ask me what he's like."

"Good thing I was there to see it," he said. I could hear his grin. "Answered all of my questions."

"Asshole."

He shrugged. "I know."

I would break his collar bone. I would dislocate his shoulders. Both of them. At once. I didn't know how but I was a fast learner. Intuitive. It wouldn't take me long to figure it out. Or I would call Junie. She would know.

"You don't get to do this to me," I said. "You don't get to show up and co-opt my night. You don't get to insert yourself into my life. We are over."

"Okay."

"Over! And there is absolutely nothing you can do about it."

"Noted."

"And it's your fault. It's all your fault. Did I use you? Did I drag your feelings out of you and try to use them against you? Use them as a way to manipulate you? Did I use sex-Did I use one of the best things we had to make you-You absolute piece of shit."

"Huh." His voice was softer. Gentler. Genuine. "That's what it was? I should have seen that."

I was ready to fly at him. To peel the skin off his face when I heard him whisper.

"Idiot. Fucking idiot."

I knew the words weren't for me. I had to dive deep to find my anger again. I had to force my fingers to grasp it.

"You have the nerve, the audacity, the balls to-"

"Take your clothes off, Cash."

I stopped. Everything in me came to a crashing halt. From my brain to my feet. And they stopped so fast I almost tripped over myself. I almost fell down. I caught myself. And heat once again suffused my body.

"What?" I hated how small I sounded.

"Take your clothes off."

"Listen to me, you piece of shit. If you think I came over here to just-"

"Isn't it? Isn't that why you came over here with your hot head and wetter pussy?"

Something in me buckled. Another thing crumbled when he stood. When he didn't turn to me. He just slid those big hands into his pockets.

"I listened. And I heard you." His voice hardened. "I heard you, Cash. And you know what happens when I hear you."

I heard you, he always said every time I fussed at him. I heard you, so I'll fix it.

"Take your clothes off."

I reached for the zipper of my dress.

CHAPTER EIGHT

Cassidy

I was closer to the door than he was to me. I knew that was on purpose. I knew he stood with the couch between us and his eyes on my reflection in his windows on purpose. So I would know that I was the reason I was naked. I would know I chose everything that happened to me next. He didn't force it. He didn't apply any pressure. I just wanted it. Wanted it enough to let him watch. Wanted it enough not to make excuses or to lay my actions at his feet.

That was why he hadn't offered me the wine when I came in. That was why I hadn't poured my own glass.

The wine was for after.

I didn't question myself. What for? Did it matter if he was right? That maybe I'd driven over in the hopes that we would cross one of the lines I drew in the sand? Did it matter that he told me to take off my clothes and I couldn't hold back the craving for him? Did anything matter except how clearly I could remember how his hands felt on me?

That I wanted it again? That I was naked and he came around the couch to me?

There was a flush on his cheeks. One that said control was hard for him, that he was too invested and incapable of pulling back. That he might hurt me the first time and wouldn't think to apologize for it until after the third time.

Thank God.

His eyes didn't leave mine. That was what made him different. That I stood naked in his home. Naked and ready. And nothing mattered more than the connection between us, nothing mattered more than building a bubble that only we existed in.

I couldn't push the air out of me fast enough. I couldn't take in enough. I-

He kissed me. His hands gripped my face to stop them from shaking. He tasted the same. Smelled the same.

Home. I was home.

He pressed close and I remembered how decadent it was to press my naked body against his clothes one. How silk-cotton blends felt against my nipples and his hard, clothed thighs felt pressed against mine. I moaned into the silence.

Hands fisted in my hair. Sharp pain when he lifted me. Pain that made me wrap my arms and legs around him and press closer. Moan again.

He stumbled to his bed and I wasn't afraid. The kiss was mine then. And I wanted it to set him on fire. I wanted it to torture him. I wanted it to make him crawl out of his own skin.

I bounced when he threw me onto the bed. I laughed when he ripped the buttons of his shirt. I gasped and sighed when he pushed my legs apart and his tongue- Insistent. Had it always been that way? No. Usually it was soft first.

Coaxing me to the first orgasm. Never rushed. Never grasping the way it was in that moment.

It was like he dragged me to that first orgasm and shoved me into it. Shoved me and then held me inside it. I tried to get away from him. I wasn't supposed to feel so much so fast. He'd never done that to me before. He was supposed to be gentler. He was supposed to-

He slapped my thigh, pulled and twisted one of my nipples, ran his teeth over my clit all at once. And it was me that wanted to crawl out of my own skin. I tried. I scratched both of us. I writhed. I screamed and begged for a mercy that I knew wasn't coming. I arched and twisted. There was no relief. Just another orgasm. And another.

My throat was too raw to say his name but I tried when he pushed inside of me. The garbled sound that came out of me didn't sound like his name. But he understood. He kissed me and whispered "Cash" into my ear. Into the candlelight that reached out to us.

I wrapped my arms around his neck and tried to bind him to me. If he was close, he would be still. I tried. He laughed and showed me what close felt like. Torture. A different kind. A new kind that made me ask him what he wanted from me.

"Everything." He sounded like the devil.

And I opened for him like a flower in spring. Like a fool. I gave him back all the places that I lied and said weren't his. Consequences and the morning after be damned.

He was worth it.

Maybe he was still mine.

I pulled the condom off and lapped up the taste of him. Sucked it off him until there nothing left but his warmth and his strangled moans. The condom he pressed into my palm when I held out my hand.

I watched him when I rode him. Laid a hand over his heart and used its beating as a guide. There he was. Like I'd left him but better because he didn't close his eyes the way he used to. He didn't bite his lip or try to hold anything back. He gave and gave until I felt an imbalance between us and rose and fell until my thighs burned to make us equals again.

I collapsed onto his chest seconds after he arched and gasped into what I gave him. I thought we would rest. But the condom was gone. Thrown to the ground. I laughed at the mess it made. At the trust he gave me. Smiled when he opened another and sighed when he was inside me again.

Fast that time. Whipped hips and the slap of skin. Scratches on his back and a hand around my throat. Tighter, tighter, until my eyes opened and focused on his. All that violence. The lack of control and yet when we came together it was quiet. Soft sighs and softer hands. His weight, hot and familiar, settled over me. I was safe.

He kissed me. "You want some wine? Let me get you some wine."

CHAPTER NINE

Cassidy

I was ready to regret it. And I was ready to do it again. Every dirty filthy moment. I floated in the place between sleep and awareness and compared Cahir to Kevin.

I stopped fucking Kevin when I found out about his wife. When I dreamed about his son and his daughter. It was a line I could have crossed. The human mind is capable of justifying anything if you give it enough time and incentive. But I didn't. Because it explained everything. The film on my skin after I fucked him. Like a coating of gasoline over my purest things. The inability to meet his eyes. I consented; there was always a feeling of shame. Of otherness. Wrongness. I avoided his eyes and convince myself that he did the same. That he felt some shame. I tried to convince myself that I wasn't wrong. We were just different. Odd.

I steeled myself for it to be that way with Cahir. I softened my thighs. Ready to part them when he reached for me. Only his hand never came. I left space between my lips. The better to welcome his kiss. But that never came either. I relaxed my body. Eased deeper into the mattress that he paid too much for but that I loved more than anything else he owned. To make it easier for him. To make it better for me-that first moment I felt his weight on mine.

But he wasn't there. I felt it. And as I drifted closer to reality, I smelled it. Eggs and bacon. I heard the toaster jump. The music we reserved for making breakfast meals together.

I smelled him. Felt him. Not the way I wanted. Not the way I dreaded.

He pushed me.

Hard.

"You're not asleep. Get the fuck up." He shoved the covers off me.

I didn't pretend. I sat straight up in bed. "This is a quality mattress. I deserve a-"

"-breakfast that isn't going to be fucking served to you in bed. You have clothes in the closet. Get up."

"Clothes?"

"I went to your apartment."

"What did you bring?" I sprang out of bed.

"Shut up."

I ran to his closet. He went back to the kitchen.

"Fuck." It was perfect. Exactly what I would have chosen. Easy and carefree. Heels high though so everyone knew that I was relaxed but not to be fucked with. And nothing matched. Not a single thing.

"I got it right?" He stood in the doorway. Naked from the waist up. A plate of food in one hand and juice in the other.

I closed my mouth for a second. Breathed through my nose. "Who helped you? Gran?"

He shook his head and I knew he didn't lie. Gran leaned towards monochrome looks. Things that billowed.

"Junie didn't help either," he said.

I knew that too even though I was going to ask. I had to lock onto a reason. I had to lock onto something that would explain what was happening in my stomach. Between my thighs.

"Hurry up," he said.

"I'm still going to have to go home for-"

"-makeup's in the bathroom."

"And I can take myself to work since-"

"I took your car back to your place. I'll take you to work like I always do."

He did always take me to work when I spent the night at his house. Even when we were friends. To give us a little more time. And my makeup was in his bathroom. With my favorite shower gel and lotions. All of my skin care products.

It didn't matter. The night before. What he did that morning. How what he did that morning felt more intimate than anything he'd ever done to me at night.

I showered. Dressed. Put on makeup. And smiled when he handed me breakfast. A wobbly smile that I straightened before he could see it or question it.

He shared the paper with me. We traded and read the stories the other found interesting. He told me things that could probably be categorized as insider trading. We laughed over the comics together.

He put on music I hadn't heard before in the car and didn't try to hold my hand. It was me that leaned toward him for a kiss that I shouldn't have expected to come. It was me that checked my cell phone once the morning rush was over. Me that didn't feel any surprise when there was a text from him. A recipe. And a question mark.

As if he had to ask. As if I had the energy to try and identify how I felt.

We made lunch together. No arms wrapped tight around my waist or kisses to my neck. No nimble, long fingers turned the stove down or off. They didn't boost me up onto the counter and encourage my clothes to leave my body or find their way to the parts of me that existed for their touch.

Just lunch. Just conversation.

Just friendship.

oo

Cahir

Success went to the one that recognized opportunity and grabbed it. It went to the person that looked beyond themselves and their ego and saw what was in front of them. That's the hardest part-getting past your own ego. Getting out of your own way.

It was the most difficult part when Cash came over that night. I didn't want to get out of my own way. I wanted to fight with her. I wanted to throw my weight and my words around. I wanted to be loud too. I wanted to tell her that no one talked to me the way I let her.

I stayed still instead. I watched her instead. I pushed my own feelings to the side to be dealt with later.

Thank God.

Beyond the anger was hurt, frustration, disappointment. Mixed in with the angry words was what I'd done to break us. Hand in hand with the frustration was longing for me. For me to fix it.

I should have seen it. I should have known. In that elevator, I should have been different, better. Should have. But in that elevator all I wanted was a weapon. All I wanted was proof that I could tell her the worst and still have her tethered to me. Of course she would see that as manipulation. Of course she would see that as a betrayal of what we built, an abuse of feelings she'd run from. She was right.

And for the first time since she told me our relationship was over I felt like I could breathe. I knew what I'd done. I knew that I could fix it. I knew that she wanted me to fix it.

When I watched her take off her clothes…when she let me touch her…when she touched me back…I knew. There was no life without her. No life that would leave me fulfilled. I needed her.

Ego said go get her. Ego said make love to her until she felt like she'd absorbed me into her skin. Until we were the same. Ego said she was mine again she just didn't know it. Touch her. Touch her until she accepted the truth. But that wouldn't work with Cash. My woman, my best friend, would need something different.

She would need me to be her friend. She would need to see that the decision was hers.

I kept my hands to myself. My thoughts to myself. My desire to myself. My amusement as she tried to figure out what the hell I was doing. My joy when after a week of texting her plans for us to hang out she text me about drinks with Junie.

I wore her favorite suit. Her favorite cologne. I left my expectations at home. And tried not to jump out of my skin every time she touched me. Like she used to. Without conscious thought. Touch that lingered. Stroked. Caressed.

I was patient. You didn't amass the kind of money I had

if you weren't, but I almost lost it. Cash could always make me feel like I was about to lose it.

I kept my eyes on her. Tried to show her what she was doing to me. She either didn't see it or didn't care. And I was positive that I wasn't going to last another five minutes in that bar without dragging her into a bathroom or a corner and doing things that would probably get us arrested.

"I'm going to go," Junie said.

I blinked. "What?"

She twisted her teal braids up into a bun. "Cassidy doesn't see it. I do. And I don't want to be here when it happens."

I didn't just laugh. I screamed with it. The desire that threatened to choke me abated just a bit.

"Exactly." Junie grinned and the men she'd ignored all night leaned in her direction. "There's a hotel close by. And you're supposed to be a patient man. That's what I heard about you."

"God, stop," I wheezed.

"I want to laugh," Cash said.

"You should be laughing," Junie said. "You're the one that did it."

"So confused," Cash said.

"I'm leaving." Junie slid her purse onto her shoulder. She rolled her eyes when I handed her the business cards she collected.

"Stay," Cash said in the voice she saved for the moments when she had to be polite but still sort of meant the words that came out of her mouth. "We don't get to hang out the three of us. And you don't even have a real reason to go."

"You've been touching him like you're fucking him and want everyone in the room to know it since he got here." Junie popped her gum and the old man beside us who didn't have a shot in hell looked like he fell in love. "He's ready to fuck you in a corner and bribe everyone in here to pretend they didn't see anything."

"Scary."

"Yes, observant women are terrifying. Figure out if you want to fuck him, Cass. Then after you fuck him call me. I saw these shoes." Junie left with a wiggle of her fingers and a pop of gum that left behind the scent of mango.

"Was she right?" Cash's hands, and her eyes, were on me.

I swallowed and knew I wasn't sure if I wanted to answer her question with words or action.

∞

Cassidy

I didn't think about it. I didn't have to. He was my Cahir. Of course I would touch him, reach for him. No, I wouldn't think about it. I didn't think about breathing or blinking or any of the other things my body had to do in order to keep me alive. I just did them.

He was beyond precious to me. He was necessary. I knew that when I got over my anger from that night. Knew that he was something that I needed to have around me. So I settled back into us, or the version of us that I could handle. I thought that was friendship. I thought it was just- But his body was a comfort to me. To know that it was there, that he was real, it soothed me. I didn't know why I needed to be soothed.

"I-I don't want you to answer that."

He grinned. I didn't realize how close my face was to his. My lips. "I know, Cash."

Of course. He knew everything about me. I shivered

and knew he noticed. His body went still then tight. Eyes brighter. And there was that flush on his cheekbones. The one that told me to run if I wanted to have any choice in where he ripped my clothes off. And was I any better? Soft to his tight. Breathless in the face of his desire and what it would mean for me. What it would make me say and do. How I would debase myself. How much I wanted to be debased. Powerless.

"Don't." His voice was rough. "You know I'll do it."

"Yes."

"Cash."

"Cahir."

"You don't want this. Not really."

"Don't tell me what I want." I trailed my fingers over his thigh and liked how I could feel the evidence of his workouts. Liked how I couldn't help but remember in vivid detail what thighs that strong were capable of doing to me.

"Ok." He captured my fingers and put them on the bar. "Why don't you tell me what you want."

"You." I was proud of and surprised by my honesty. By how easy it was to cross back over the line I drew in spite of all the things that were between us.

"And after that?" He was so close I could feel his lips move over mine.

He did it on purpose. Clever man. Crafty man. Lips that made me think of sin and words that made me...think.

"After that I-" I shrugged.

"Maybe," God, I could get high on his voice alone. Come from his voice alone. "Maybe before I drag you into corners and bathrooms and cars and your place and mine and alleys and brick walls-maybe before we do that you tell me what you want to have happen to us after."

"Why?"

"Because I'm not going to be the friends with benefits

guy while you keep dating around in the hopes that you find someone who can do for you what I do. All or nothing, Cash." He dropped a soft kiss to my lips. Was it supposed to be my reminder that dating was futile? That nothing would be better than him? He stood and dropped money on the bar. "You had more to drink than me. Let me take you home."

CHAPTER TEN

Cahir

I wished for eternal sunshine and warm weather when I saw Cash. For a lifetime of whatever mood she was in when she decided that one of my t-shirts, a leather jacket, and thigh high boots was the best thing to wear to the farmer's market.

I stuffed my hands into my pockets. "You look great."

"You have great taste in t-shirts." She kissed my cheek.

"Are you-" I sniffed again. "Are you wearing my cologne?"

"It smells better on me, right?"

"You aren't playing fair, Cash."

She laughed and looped her arm through mine. I took the basket I bought her on our first farmer's market trip our of her hand. We wandered for a while. Just to get an idea of what was there, what we could make, what we had a taste for. Then we started shopping.

"Would it be ridiculous if I got more succulents?" She ran her fingers over them.

"I hope not. I bought a pallet of them for you before you got here."

"Cahir!"

"That's what happens when you're late." I shrugged and steered her away from the plants.

"Is that criticism or encouragement?"

I laughed. "Why don't you tell me why you're trying to kill me?"

"What do you mean?" Her eyes were wide. Eyelashes fluttered.

I loved her.

I gestured to her outfit. "Come on. You're dressed for war."

"I have questions." She chewed on her bottom lip. "About Zion."

My hand tightened around hers. I stopped in a patch of sunlight that made her eyes more than miraculous. They were otherworldly. "It's me, Cash. Me. You don't have to do anything to get the truth from me but ask. I'm sorry I made you doubt that."

"Don't be kind. It doesn't make me feel like less of an asshole."

"Fine." I rolled my shoulders. "How dare you have perfectly natural questions for me, you meddlesome bitch. What do you think we are? Friends? Best friends?"

Her mouth fell open and for a second we stood in silence. A long second that made me wonder if this was the thing that would make her punch me in the face.

She laughed. "Now I don't feel like an asshole. Thanks."

"Anything for you." Did she know how much I meant that? "Ask."

"Have you seen her? Been to appointments?"

If there were any doubts in my mind that Zion wasn't

the one for me, that I was finished, the nausea that rose up in me would have laid them to rest.

"You wanna know something interesting?"

"Hmm?" She ran her fingers over produce. Selected the best ones.

"You're the first and only person in my life that asks the real questions. The ones that prove you're paying attention to me, that you want to know."

She looked up. "No one's asked you if you've gone to a doctor's appointment? What kind of self-absorbed assholes do you have around you?"

"We like talking about work and money."

"Kids don't affect money?"

"Touché"

"So?"

It was easier because she didn't look at me. "I haven't seen her. I-It's kind of pathetic."

"No." She threw more vegetables in the basket. Still didn't look at me. "It's not."

I loved her. My best friend. "I'm scared to see her."

"What brings the fear?"

"Anger." I felt heavier and lighter for admitting it to her. For the way she didn't react, just waited.

"Tell me about it."

I let out a shuddering breath and walked with her to the next stall. Let her drag me. "I was proud of myself for ending it, for staying away. Proud of myself for rebuilding my life, getting myself back. Falling in love with you."

She squeezed my hand.

"I was thinking about my future. No. Past thinking about it. I was planning it. And it was good, Cash. Real fucking good."

"Of course it was. It's what you deserve."

Didn't she know I would fuck her in front of the squash if she said things like that?

"She took my future from me. I didn't know she could take anything else from me. I didn't know I could feel... violated again. Once was enough. Dreaming it every night was enough. Scars on my knuckles. I thought I was over with it. Done. Then O'Shea tells me and I'm feeling it all over again. Every second."

"Cahir."

"Only this time I'm angry. Because she succeeded. She got pregnant. She got a way to pull me back into her life and make me fell like I'm the bottom of the fucking barrel again. How does she do that?"

"I-"

"And then the guilt hits. Because there's a baby. An innocent life that has fuck-all to do with all this shit. Didn't even ask to be in this shit. Just got thrown in it. That's what I should be focused on. My child. Not her bullshit. I should be focused on becoming a father. And I can't."

"You can do both."

"What?"

"You can be excited about your child and have feelings about the mother."

"Zion's not going to be my kid's mother." The words were sharper than I meant them to be. But Cash had to know.

"Okay." She rubbed my arm. "Okay. You can feel how you want about Zion and be excited about the baby. You can chew gum and walk."

I laughed. She could always make me laugh. And once I finished laughing, I always realized she was right.

∞

Cassidy

I was love and light. I was the culmination of my ancestors's hopes and dreams. The best of them. I was the best and worst of Black women. An individual not a monolith. I was a whole and healed person.

That Cahir was angry with Zion, over her, wouldn't go back to her to form a perfect family, shouldn't have made me so happy.

An ugly kind of happy. The kind that feels twisted from its inception because it takes pleasure in another's loss. But I couldn't help it. I didn't want to step away from it. I wallowed in it. And every second felt like going to the spa until I remembered that I was supposed to be better, that Cahir deserved better of his friends.

I sat on my couch with my amethyst in my palms and closed my eyes. I opened my mind. It was still water. An endless expanse of still water that contained nothing that would hurt me. Only things that would welcome me. I breathed deep. In. Out. And dove beneath the surface to see what there was to be seen without judgment.

Love. Bright and steady and unable to be ignored. For so many. And wasn't that beautiful? That I had so many people in my life that I could share my love with? That I could love them in a way that spoke to them? And they loved me. In a way that resonated. Given and received. It was what gave me light.

There was my love for Cahir. A bit brighter. A bit different in feel. I dove deeper into it and it lost its clean, its shine. Murky and gritty. And I knew that was my own fault. I could see it.

I could see the anxiety and insecurity, the anger. Could see how they made what was once so beautiful less.

I gathered them close in my mind and held them the

way my physical body held the crystal and examined them. It would have been easier, my mind whispered to me, to leave them alone. Or to hand responsibility of them to him. Cahir could be the reason I felt the way he did. And I could let the anxiety and the insecurity turn to anger and bitterness because he didn't see them and so didn't fix them. It would be easier.

It would make our love different. Loving Cahir was so unique, so special, so valuable because it was the first love that was wholly my own. I grew it. I tended it. I mended and amended it. I carried it. And he carried his own love. He made sure it was right for him and safe for me. I owed him the same.

I owed myself honesty. The honest truth was there had always been something about Zion. I still didn't know what she looked like. I avoided O'Shea's paintings and photographs online. I stayed far away from her favorite spots after Junie told me what they were. And I didn't look for her amongst Cahir's things.

I thought that when I knew her I would lose a piece of myself. The piece that was confident. The piece that was content. The piece that was solid and sure and steady. The piece that thought I was enough for Cahir.

Because I heard. When he and Zion were together I heard about them from my clients. They were that couple. Or one of them. It seemed every time one of the New Money Girls took a man the entire City worked itself into a lather.

I heard and wondered if anyone talked about Cahir and I that way or wondered if I were a ghost of a replacement. A clean up woman. Did I pale in comparison to her? Would I break when I saw her? Would I immediately recognized that I wasn't enough? She ran a business and men's wallets?

She wanted more and I wanted a house full of plants. Designer clothes while I traipsed around in Cahir's t-shirt.

Would he ever love me the way he loved her? In a way that forced him to stop existing in a quiet way? Aunt LeAndra and Uncle Tony loved each other that way. Gran loved her husband, the one that died so young, that way even though she always knew she wouldn't have him long. I never wanted to love anyone that way. I never wanted to look up and realize that love smothered me instead of freed me. I never wanted to see that part of me was just carrying someone else.

The anxiety that maybe he would go made me mean. Made me wish he would disparage her more. Made me wish he would call her names and insult her. Would let the anger whip and cut and slice. It never did. So I was left alone for the anxiety to take root.

I shook my head and opened my eyes. It took a few minutes for me to find my phone.

Cahir answered on the first ring. "Cash."

"I'm ready to talk," I said. I thought I heard him give a quiet, little gasp. "About us."

"I'm on my way."

CHAPTER ELEVEN

Cassidy

"Let's go." He leaned against my front door and put his hands in his pockets when I would have preferred to have them on me.

I looked down at my joggers and athletic slides. "Where?"

"You forget this is your normal feeding time?"

I laughed. There was nothing nearby I felt comfortable throwing at him. "Wait."

He sighed. Dramatic and long. "You look great. We can just go."

"The lies you tell." I went to my closet.

He followed me. "No. If you do it, we'll be here forever and you'll ask a million questions that don't matter. And then I'll be hungry too. Do the tiara thingy with your hair."

"The what?"

"With the braid" He made a circle around the top of his head.

"A what?"

He gestured to my closet. "I have important things to figure out. The one big braid that goes around in a loop or whatever."

"A crown braid?" I bit my lip.

"If I knew what it was really called we wouldn't be having this chat, would we?"

"It's a crown braid."

"Whatever. You're an awful client to style. You never follow directions." He disappeared into my closet. "Questions, questions, questions. Just do what I said."

He heard me laugh. I know he did. He just didn't respond.

I did my hair. He laid an outfit on my bed. I looked at it.

"I have a purse-"

He waved a hand. "Who's the stylist here?"

"Oh. So sorry."

"Forgiven." He came back a moment later with the purse I thought was the best choice for the outfit.

"It's scary that you can do that." I stripped and put on what he picked out and didn't know how I felt about how respectful he was.

I didn't know if I liked that he looked at his phone instead of at my body.

"Do what?"

"Dress me."

"It's just paying attention."

"No. It isn't."

A small smile played over his lips. It grew a little when I twirled in front of him.

"You're really beautiful, you know." He kissed each of my fingers and I forgot how to breathe.

"Thank you."

"Thank you." He winked and linked our fingers.

He took us to a barbecue spot that had bourbon cocktails on tap. Six of them.

"I'm in trouble," I said.

"We're going to get all of them. At once. And share them." He didn't look up from the menu. "Should we get ribs and chicken or go wild and try the brisket? No. Don't say it."

I closed my mouth.

"We're too far north for you to eat brisket, right? Does Mother's have brisket?"

"I love you," I said.

"It's been four weeks and three days since you said that to me." He kept his eyes on the menu. Voice almost a murmur.

"That's it? You don't know it down to the-"

"-six hours and fifteen minutes. Don't play with me, Cash."

I laughed. I laughed so much with him. "I love you. And I have no idea what Zion looks like. I'm terrified that if I see her I'll shrivel up inside and run screaming because I'm not her."

His hand was heavy when it settled over mine. The way blankets and my parent's love were. Warm. Solid. Constant. He ordered dinner, the right dinner, and turned his attention back to me. It was there in the simple things, the little things. They were what held all the reasons why I couldn't make it past the first date with anyone else.

"I'm going to tell you this every day for the rest of our lives if I have to. You ready?"

The rest of our lives…I nodded and wished for water.

"Zion is Zion. You are you. She was a part of my life I'm never going back to. You're the part of my life I'm never giving up." His thumb rubbed circles on my palm. "Trying to avoid Zion is like me trying to avoid Kevin."

I snorted.

"Yeah." He tilted his head. "At least I think so. That's ridiculous to you, right? Cause I'm obviously the better choice?"

There was a joke in there about both of them hiding babies from me but the spirit of discernment settled on my shoulders and made me nod.

"Zion was wild and dangerous and someone from the outside looking in would have said it was glamorous and fated and all these other cute words that don't mean shit. She wasn't good for me, Cash. She wasn't forever."

I was glad he stopped. Glad all he had for me was a steady gaze that said there was more if I was ready for it.

I wasn't. "Tell me. Tell me what life would be like if I stayed with you. If I was with you."

He leaned forward. Ready.

I raised a hand. "I think about it. A lot. And I have to tell you, before you start, that if it's anything but being a real part of your life, a constant part, I can't do it. If I'm hidden away in the corner while you try to coparent with Zion-"

"-Zion isn't raising my kid."

There was no reason for me to translate what was in his eyes. What I thought was in his heart. Some places were too deep for me to swim.

"If I'm around your kid, I'm going to love it like I love you. I am. It would have to be permanent for me."

"Do you know what you're saying?"

"Yes. And no." I sighed. "I know what I want to say. And I know what saying it means. But-"

"-okay. Don't say it then. Not until you're ready. But, Cash?"

"Hmm?"

"When you do say it…" The smile grew slow across his face. Slow and predatory.

CHAPTER TWELVE

Cassidy

I didn't mean to stay late. But I had an idea. A piece of an idea. I knew it was good. Knew it would make me and Delia richer than we had any business to be. So I curled into the couch in the office with only lamplight to keep me company and made graphs, projections- conservative and ridiculous. And I was excited. There was nothing, absolutely nothing, like making cash money. I laughed and reached for my phone to call Cahir, to tell him about my idea, to hear what he thought of it.

"Hi, Cassidy."

My grin got a little wider. "I was wondering how long it would take you to make your way in here."

"I had to be sure Cahir did his job before I did mine."

I liked O'Shea. I liked the transformation that she went through. I'd followed her style. From when she ran the restaurant that crashed and burned without her to leaving Domingo to finding and marrying Guy. It was beautiful to watch her blossom and settle into her own skin, her clothes, her pregnancy. She sat down next to me on the couch.

I closed my laptop and twisted my body to face hers. "He told me you're pregnant. Congratulations."

"Delia didn't tell you? She's supposed to be shouting my news from the rooftops the way Nadia is."

"With the way she feels about pregnancy? We had a woman that wanted us to style her for her maternity shoot, and I thought Delia was going to throw her over the railing."

She laughed. A masculine sound. I always thought that was why O'Shea got away with so many of the things, and people, she did. She carried an easy blend of masculinity and femininity that made you feel like she wasn't like you, she wasn't competition. "Did he tell you the rest of it?"

"Zion." My smile fell. "I'm sorry. I know hearing she's pregnant must be hard for you."

"Huh. Didn't expect you to apologize to me."

"She's your-"

"No. She isn't."

"Oh." Would everyone be so sharp when they told me Zion wasn't a part of their lives? That the bonds were broken?

She pressed a hand to her stomach. "What will you do?"

"What am I supposed to do?"

"Too easy. Don't deflect."

"Damn." I chuckled. "That usually works."

"I'm sure."

"If I stay, I'll love the baby. That's what babies do. They wrap themselves around you, make you their slaves. I'll want to be a part of the baby's life. Forever." I didn't know why I opened my mouth and told so much of the truth. Didn't know if she would care or could see.

"If you stay for the baby, you have to stay for Cahir, forever."

"Can I be ready for forever? I love him. But forever? Right now? And why aren't you pissed?"

"Let's start at the top." She slid her fingers between mine and the smile bloomed across my face again. "Ximena taught me about forever. She said you can't fathom forever. And what you can't fathom you can't plan for. So don't worry about it. Worry about that day. And the day after that. Because that's all forever is: a series of todays. It took me a while to understand and a bit longer to see she was right. Today and tomorrow. That's it. Can you see yourself with him today? Can you see yourself with him tomorrow? What about the next tomorrow and the one after that? Will he still fit when things are jagged? Will he fit when they're so smooth they're slippery? Will he cling to you in the storms and smile, positive that you'll do well, when you have to walk the road alone? Is he your best friend? The one that sees the ugly and says you're beautiful?"

Tears gathered under my eyes. It was O'Shea that wiped them away. "God, you're such an artist. So many words."

She laughed.

"Zion. If she had fought for him instead of herself, if she had done everything she could to heal them and repair them, if she had respected his love, if she had done all that and he left her for you, I would have torn him apart. I would have ripped you into your smallest pieces and ground you into dust." The laughter was gone. Truth. Just truth remained. "But she didn't fight for his love. She didn't fight for mine. What am I going to do? Hate the woman that would fight? Hate the woman willing to turn her life upside down because she's smart enough to respect a miracle and be gentle with it when she gets it?"

I nodded and wiped away her tears.

"I say it because I need to be strong. I say she isn't my sister because I need to let go and everything in me is rebelling against it. But she is my sister. More than that she's a part of me. So that baby is too. It's just as much my kid as the one I'm carrying. Delia and Nadia would say the same. Can you be comfortable with us being there? With us being a part of your life forever?"

I hadn't thought of that. Hadn't considered that it wouldn't be just Cahir that I would have to keep. Cahir and the baby wouldn't be the only new members of my family. I- There were too many things. Too many things.

But as always, when it felt like the world was a little too much, there was a Black woman holding my hand. Ready to be a comfort or a shield or whatever else I needed. I twisted on the couch and laid my head on O'Shea's shoulder and enjoyed the quiet with her.

∞

Cassidy

"I'm going to ask you for something crazy." I leaned against Junie's desk.

"Do you know who we work with?" Junie popped her gum. "I doubt it."

"Really? What do they ask you for?"

"Recently? Dynamite. But Guy came over and shut it down before I could get more details."

"Dyna-No. I don't want to know. But that is kind of what I want to ask about."

"Explosives? Cause I'll tell you like I told O'Shea, C-4 is more sophisticated, cleaner, and easier for me to get my hands on."

"How?"

"I grew up in Strawberry Fields. Mr didn't clean it up that much."

I laughed and grabbed a piece of gum out of her desk. "I need to talk to Guy. Is there a way for you to find out where he is?"

She picked up her phone. "Want me to text you the address or what?"

"You have his location?"

"I'm the emergency contact for every single person in this building and the men they with. Yes. I have locations."

"Emergency contact?"

"Well." She flipped highlighter orange braids over her shoulder. "I would be if they had any sense."

"You hacked their phones?"

"I designated myself as their safety monitor. You want the address or not?"

The address Junie gave me led me to a hotel. Or at least the sign said it would be a hotel. One day. I parked and got out of the car. A stocky man jogged up to me.

"Press aren't supposed to come until tomorrow."

I smiled. "I'm not with the press. I'm here to see Guy? Could you tell him-"

"-he's married. Happily. His wife's pregnant."

"Yes, I know. I work at Beyond with her. Could you tell him Cassidy is here?"

"You're a friend of O'Shea's?"

"She's backed me into a couple corners." I shrugged.

He laughed. "Yeah. You know her. Come on."

He got me a hardhat and led me through the noise of tools and men yelling to Guy who was busy with a jackhammer.

"Boss." A finger was jerked towards me.

The jackhammer went quiet and my ears rang from the

sudden absence of noice. Gloves like catcher's mitts and oversized glasses fell away.

"Cassidy?"

"Hey, Guy." It occurred to me how awkward this whole thing was. He didn't know me, and I didn't know him. And what was I even there to say? "There's nothing wrong with O'Shea or anything."

"I know." He motioned for me to follow him over to a makeshift table covered with plans and pulled out a chair for me. "Junie would call me if there was. We have an agreement after-Anyways."

"Yeah."

"So you're here for you. And Cahir. Talk to me about it."

"I had things to say but now-" I shook my head. "It made sense in the car."

"Always makes sense during the drive." He nodded.

I liked him. Had always liked him. My father loved football and told me about Guy. Showed me highlight reels and explained in careful words and tones why Guy was one of the best things to happen to the City both on and off the field. He even did business with him. Brought him into Baltimore real estate development and restoration and said Guy was the best rival he had.

But I didn't know him. And I showed up to tell him what?

"I knew who Domingo was when I fell in love with O'Shea." Guy laughed. The way Southern men did. In a way that said they had time and a secret supply of sunshine.

"Really?"

"I ate at Domingo's restaurant for Tony and I's amuse-ment. Domingo hated us so we showed up in the one place he couldn't just come out and be a dick. I wanted to go home that particular night. I remember that. The men I was eating with were gossiping about O'Shea, reminding why I didn't like Domingo. I saw her out the corner of my eye and just-Forgot she existed for two years? Sort of?"

"Really?" I was a broken record, but really? They seemed...made for each other. That it hadn't been some love at first sight thing was a little past shocking and close to ridiculous.

"So I come out the security room at The Club because someone's in the hall cackling like a hyena, and it's her. And I knew an O'Shea was taking over but I thought it was some Irish guy or some shit. It's her. And she's looking at me." He smiled. Easy with the memory. "She's smiling. Flirting. Her hand's in mine. And she is mine. I see that. The moment I come in the hall. She's mine, and there's something that's getting in the way of me getting what I want."

I held my breath. I didn't tell him but he understood. He knew why I was there.

"He's right there. Every interaction we have. And I'm holding myself back just a little bit because yeah, I love her. Crazy kind of thing that goes past love and-"

"I get it."

"Of course you do." His smile was kind. He leaned back in the chair and didn't seem alarmed by the sounds it made. "So I'm basically obsessed. I'd walk around with a knife between my ribs if it amused her. And I've never felt like this before, right? She's it. All wrapped up in one. And she can't be mine because she's got an abusive ex that won't go away."

"How did you do it?"

"You mean how do I do it? Yeah, he'll never physically show up, but he's still there. She'll be about to do or say something and she has to stop because whatever it was- wasn't for me. She was reacting to him."

"How?"

"The scars Zion left will never go away. The memory of her will never go away. You'll walk in a room, and he'll be there, and you'll just know she's on his mind. Not like he's pining for her. It's just a road he has to walk sometimes. Let him walk it." He braced his elbows on his knees. "And set up some boundaries for yourself. Figure out how much is okay for you. How much you can let slide and how much is too much before you have to get away and take care of you. Don't ever stop taking care of you."

"I-I can do that?"

"Without boundaries how do you stop yourself from becoming the next victim?"

"Wow. That was way more profound than I expected it to be."

He laughed and shrugged. "You can do this thing however you want. I lucked out. I got to make sure Domingo never walks again. You'll find something that works for you."

"I think I already have," I said.

He nodded and let me wander off. I eventually found my way to my car and thought it was time to go see Cahir.

CHAPTER THIRTEEN

Cahir

I used to call myself patient, willing to lie in wait for what I wanted until it was there, right there and so easy to come by it wouldn't make sense not to go for it. I used to say I had tenacity.

I spent a week feeling like a fucking coward. Again. I could see it. It was all over Cash. She had something to say. Something that would change things. Something that would twist and turn us into something new all over again. I knew and didn't say a word. Let her sit on it. Simmer with it. Prayed against all hope that she would say something when she was ready and I wouldn't have to drag it out of her.

We watched a movie, a scary one for her. In the middle of the day for me. She laughed and I jumped which made her laugh harder and made things seem more right between us. Comfortable. I missed that when she was gone. It wasn't until I had her that I realized I'd never been really comfortable with anyone in my life.

"Can we talk about something?"

I took a deep breath and grinned like I wasn't strung tighter than a racist at a Black Lives Matter rally. "Whatever you want."

"I've been thinking a lot about what your future is going to look like. When the baby comes. And where I want to be in it." She turned on the sofa until she faced me. A tangle of limbs and a crown of curls.

"Okay."

"And what I'm about to propose is kind of terrifying. Why are you smiling?"

I shook my head. "Say it."

"I know you. At least I think I do."

"You know me."

"Okay." She laughed a little. "You say that Zion isn't going to raise your kid. She isn't going to be your kid's mother. But you've never said that your kid won't have a mother."

So she had been paying attention.

"I knew what you meant. The first time you said it, I knew what you meant. I knew what you wanted. And I thought you'd lost your fucking mind."

I nodded. If I were her, I would have thought the same thing.

"You-The elevator broke something in me. Or it broke something about who I thought we were to each other. Who I thought we were together." She tilted her head. "I've forgiven you for it. Because I know you understand. But that doesn't mean I'm better. Not all the way."

When I reached out, she put her hand in mine. It didn't fix everything, it didn't fix anything, but it soothed me and that was enough in the moment.

"I just-" She shook her head and laughed. "I'm going to love you for the rest of my life. I can see that. You're going to be more than a friend to me. You're going to be family.

So, it terrifies the shit out of me, but I want to do this with you. I want to raise that baby with you."

Maybe I moved too fast when I snatched her from her spot on the sofa and into my lap. My hands might have pulled too hard on her hair. I might have bit instead of kissed. But she was there, and she was going to be the mother of my baby. She was going to help me build a family. Something I could be proud of.

"Cahir." She turned her face. That was fine. There was her ear. Her neck. "Stop."

I went still. When she pushed against my arms, I let them fall. She stood.

"I want the baby. I want to raise the baby with you. But relationship...I'm not ready to be the nuclear family and be a married couple or even be back in a relationship with you. I'm not. The broken parts aren't fixed yet."

I stared at her.

"Cahir, did you hear me?"

"Yes."

"What did I say?"

"You're not ready to be in a relationship with me again."

"Okay."

"Okay."

She just stood there. Wrung her hands and bit the corner of her lip. She was adorable.

"Why are you still wearing clothes?"

She burst into laughter and pulled her shirt over her head.

CHAPTER FOURTEEN

Cassidy

Not a relationship. But there was love between us, and I didn't know why I denied myself. He kissed me before the laughter died on my lips. Swallowed it and the sigh that followed and then my feet weren't on the ground. It did something to me every time he picked me up and moved with me as if I weighed nothing.

Mouth on mine. His mouth never left mine. Even when he whispered that he loved me. That I'd made him so happy. That he was going to fuck me in ways that embarrassed me in the morning.

God, yes.

His hands dove deep down the back of my pants to grip my ass. To squeeze and scratch lines that would leave heat and red marks behind. I welcomed it. Threw my head back and closed my eyes to embrace it. He bit my neck. My shoulders. He set me on my feet.

My clothes were gone. So were his. Middle of the day

and I couldn't see where my clothes had gone. I couldn't see at all. I could only hear. And feel.

"Can I tell you the truth?" He didn't wait for my response. He was smart enough to know I couldn't find my words. "The happier you make me the more I want to hurt you."

I felt wetness slide and dance an uneven path down my thigh.

"Can I hurt you a little? Surprise you?"

My head was on his shoulder. I nodded.

"I need to hear you say yes, Cash." His tongue traced the shell of my ear. "I'm going to need to hear it a lot."

"Yes." I didn't recognize my own voice.

I didn't recognize his bed though I'd spent so many nights in it. That was a gift of his. He could twist my desire and his voice to make the world a brand new place that I didn't want to explore because I was so wrapped up in him.

He spread me wide, wider than I thought my legs would go, then put my hands on my knees. "Hold them."

I heard the nightstand drawers open and smiled. I bought some things. Threw them in beside the condoms.

"I like that you bought these." Buzzing noises filled my ears. He dragged a vibrator down my chest and let it rest on my stomach. "I don't know how much you will."

He slid a finger inside me and then in my mouth. Moaned when I cleaned every trace of myself from his finger and said, "More, please."

He always gave me what I wanted.

The vibrator slid inside me. Thought that would be it. It was enough. A fat, curved thing that pressed and nudged into my G-spot with an insistence that surprised me. I thought I would get comfortable with it. Then his hand came down on my clit.

My body jumped like it'd been electrocuted. Twisted

and arched and my legs tried to close because his mouth was where his hands had been. His mouth wasn't what I knew it to be- insistent but always gentle. In the past it brought only pleasure. Always.

That was beyond too much. It was uncomfortable. Where there should have been only pleasure he introduced pain. He made me twist, and push, and reach, and the moment the pain felt like it could morph into something close to a friend there was his hand. And when I eased into the electricity that came with his hand when it connected to my clit over and over again, he used his fingers.

Deaf, blind, almost mute. There was only his name to say. Growl. Pant. Moan. I pleaded and promised with it. I tried to barter and found he'd already taken everything I would have offered.

Cool air clung to the sweat on my body, to the tears that pooled in and around my ears. It did nothing to quench the dryness in my throat. His sheets stuck to my back, rose and fell when I did as if convinced their new purpose was to be my second skin. And it was the middle of the day. I knew it was the middle of the day. And I knew everything around me was dark.

I thought he would stop. I thought he would have to. Eventually I would drown him. Instead he added his teeth to the torture and I gave up screaming. I howled.

"There it is." His mouth was gone. The vibrator.

I throbbed. Pussy, clit, legs, hands. The muscles in my back and thighs. God. God. Then he pinched my clit one more time and I rose off that bed. Proved that soreness and sweat and burned vocal chords and parched, dry mouths didn't matter as much as doing what Cahir said.

He was inside me. It wasn't slow like it normally was. He always gave me time. To adjust. To savor. Then he surprised me. He always held a little of himself back to surprise me with. Sometimes I thought he did it to humble me. The thought always curled my toes and made me wetter for him.

That time, there was no time, no surprise. He gave me all of him at once and made sure I knew. His hand behind my neck pulled me forward, curled me in on myself so I could see the way my body took him, could see his hips grind into me.

He kept that hand on my neck until I propped myself up on my elbows. Every time I tried to look at him, to feel like I was still with him despite how new it all was, he pushed my head back down.

"Pay attention," he said.

So I did. To the way my body moved closer to his to accept his punishing pace. To how I sounded, how he sounded, how we sounded together. To the way my hands held my knees back, and his fingers squeezed into my thighs.

He trailed a finger over my clit. I hissed.

He smiled. "Does it hurt?"

I nodded.

"Say it."

"Yes."

"Hurt it some more."

"Cahir-"

"Good. You know my name, and you heard what I said. Do it. Before I do."

My lightest touch hurt. And it left me wishing for more. I rubbed circles, figure 8's, traced stars. And I cried. Because it all felt so good. I sobbed with it. And he leaned close to me:

"You're so beautiful like this."

"Pretty girl. Pretty Cash."

"Your tears taste almost as good as your pussy."

That was when I exploded. When I lost it. My God. Fucking God.

∞

Cassidy

He held me until my tears subsided. He gave me water and wiped my body with a warm cloth. And when I enjoyed that too much he put me in his shower, on the bench, and turned on the steam settings. My body melted.

He washed me. My hair. Conditioned and detangled it. I taught him how. I didn't teach him how to be soft with me. Gentle. I had to hold back tears for a different reason.

He wrapped me in towels and then his shirt and that was better. I collected those shirts and wore them. Believed they were never-ending hugs from him. He knew. He had to. He saw everything else I did. He understood it before I did.

We laid in his bed and just breathed together. We twined hand and legs and feet around each other and smiled. He brought us food when my stomach growled. I turned on music when I knew it wouldn't offend the silence or break the moment. We used the shadows to track the hours that slipped away from us. It was perfect.

Then he started talking.

He smiled at me and tangled his fingers in my curls as he talked about the house we would buy. Or a condo even. That would be okay as long as there was some green space. The car I would need. He wanted to buy me a new car anyways, and what did I think of Range Rovers? Would I prefer a driver? And the trust fund. The baby would need a trust fund. A college fund. His parents wanted to handle the college fund but he didn't know how I felt about it. How did I feel about it?

I didn't have to open my mouth to answer. He asked about baby proofing and what I thought my grandmother would say. Shit. Gran. My parents.

Private or public schools? Home school? A nanny? What other languages should the baby learn? What books should we read to it? What were his favorite books as a baby? He'd have to call his mother.

I laid there with him as night deepened around us and wondered if Cahir were just deaf or if he was dumb too.

CHAPTER FIFTEEN

Cassidy

Gran was surrounded by flowers when I walked into the back room of her store. "I wondered when you would get here."

"When I was needed," I said and stepped around buckets and pails to get to her and lay a kiss on her cheek.

She snorted. "Sometimes you open your mouth and my words come out."

"You said it was how I would know I was a grown woman."

"Imagine my horror when I opened my mouth and my mother's opinion came flying out."

We both laughed.

"We're drying these," she said.

I sat with her on her work bench and helped her gather handfuls of lavender, then marigold, then echinacea, yarrow, and cornflower together and wrap them with twine. They would hang from the ceiling of the shop until they were dry and find their way into lotions, oils, teas, little bags to slide under a pillow or wear beneath a shirt.

She hummed as we worked. Songs that must have had lyrics but that I never heard. When humming wasn't enough she opened her mouth to let the sound come through and that was better. That was home in a deep down way that no other place or moment had been until Cahir came.

"I'm going to be a mother," I said.

"You're not pregnant."

"No." I laughed.

"And so?"

I told her the story. From beginning to end. And I never worried if it would be okay or if she would judge me because she never once stopped her humming.

"And so?"

I laughed again. Everything had to have a point with Gran. "And so I'm crazy, right? I'm agreeing to have a child with a man I'm not sure I can be in a relationship with."

"What is a family?"

"Huh?"

"What is a family?"

"People that-" I stopped. I wanted to say people that were related to each other. But I was adopting. Blood wasn't going to link me to my child. It didn't have to. "People that…"

"I think that life has been about the choices. When your grandfather passed on, Sylvia and Annette made the decision to move in close to me. They became as much mother to your father and uncles as I was." She waited for me to acknowledge the women I called and believed were my aunties, pillars of my family. "Your grandfather's brothers and sisters and cousins came in close to me."

I nodded. My and Gran's house were always full. I was

dizzy with it sometimes. And I learned not to ask who was my "real" relative, how we were related. "Family is family, ain't it?" Dozens of cousins without knowing if they really were. I only knew I was expected to fight if they did. To defend them until I fell.

"Those women you work with. They call themselves sisters and have only known each other as adults. But are they wrong?"

I didn't bother to answer something so obvious.

"I think you have to think too about what it means to be a mother. To be a good mother. Is that about the romantic relationship you have with the father? Do you have to be romantically tied to the father? Or respect him? Agree with him to love your child?"

She left me with the questions and hummed for us. We gathered so many flowers around and between us that I couldn't see her. I couldn't see the door or the floor.

She stood when we were finished and raised her arms high above her head. "Thank you, baby. Maybe next time you come we'll talk about what's really bothering you."

I was supposed to laugh. I couldn't. I went to my apartment, laid across my bed, and knew sleep wasn't coming.

∞

Cahir

I wanted every minute of every day to involve her and knew it was crazy. Crazy to want it and crazier to fight it. She let me come close. She let me talk, dream. Sometimes she smiled. Others she laughed. When I dreamed, it was rare that she talked.

She talked about the elevator. Cross-legged on my couch she talked about how she lost her friend a split second before she lost her lover and how new that was for her. She talked about how pride was what gave her the strength to walk and talk and hear. Pride and a little ego maybe.

"I remember I thought 'Of course. Of course she's pregnant. They can't have a love story that ends. She can't just let him be mine.'"

She gave a little laugh. When she talked about the elevator, when her eyes slipped from mine to stare a memory down, I never smiled. I never laughed. I listened.

I never apologized. Not after the first time. She knew. She knew every other thought I had. She didn't need to know that my grief and regret for hurting her traveled with me everywhere. Tucked in my wallet. Nestled among my keys. Shuffled in with work papers and proposals.

I listened. When she was quiet, I was. When she waited, I spoke.

I gave her an apology. To give her another would be condescending. Would be empty. What would she do with words she already had? How would they heal the wounds she tore open for me to examine the truth of?

I talked about Zion. The reality of her and me and our relationship and why it was over. Why I couldn't go back. Why it wasn't really a love story.

"Love doesn't drown you. Love doesn't leave you wondering where in the fuck all the air is and when you're gonna get back to it. Love isn't hiding or deciding not to talk or that you're just going to ask for forgiveness instead of permission." I took a deep breath. "Love isn't what happened in that elevator."

I felt her jolt. "I get that. You taught me that. I'm sorry the lesson was necessary. But I got it. I don't have any secret spots or corners or whatever that you can't get in to. No skeletons."

She nodded and lay in my arms.

Okay. Okay.

I talked to her. Constantly. Not about the baby. About my fears. About how it felt to not have her. How it felt when she came back. The weird place we were in. How I'd stay in that place for as long as she needed. That it was enough that she agreed to be friend and family and kiss me and touch me and cook dinner with me and dance to the beat while we sang off-key. That we could have as many conversations as she needed. She didn't have to be sure of me in a day.

"Guy told me he and O'Shea are taking a baby prep class," she said one night over Vin Santo and cookies.

It seemed best for me to stay quiet.

"I signed us up for it." She didn't meet my eyes when she said it. But she smiled.

She smiled.

I made love to her until she cried that night.

∞

Cassidy

I didn't know what day the excitement arrived, but it did. It wasn't the baby prep class. It wasn't the dinner with his parents. It wasn't the dinner with mine. It wasn't the pictures from the ultrasounds that Cahir got from Fine because he still couldn't see Zion. It was just…

I woke up on a Saturday and shook him awake.

He didn't open his eyes; he reached for me. "I'm not going to the farmer's market. The plants are taking over."

I laughed. "What's the correlation?"

"I always buy you more when we go there."

"I never ask."

"You look happy." He pulled me down on the bed. "Why wouldn't I give you what makes you happy?"

My mouth was busy for a while. For a while his fingers yanked my hair. His eyes slid closed but only for a few moments. His mouth fell open with his groans and whispered words.

When I was done and I kissed him until I was sure he knew what he tasted like, his lips curled in a lazy grin. "We can go to the farmer's market, Poison Ivy."

I laughed until I cried. "I don't wanna. I wanna shop for baby stuff."

His hand was tight on my wrist. Laziness was replaced with intensity and the closeness of his body. "What?"

We said we didn't want a baby shower. I hated the games. He hated people. And he said he had enough money; it wouldn't hurt him to buy a nursery full of shit. What he didn't buy our parents would trample over each other to get. Or Gran and I would make.

"Baby stuff." I smiled.

The sheets were gone and the cool air he insisted on was a shock to my skin. He-well, he didn't run, but it was close. He disappeared into the closet and was back in a moment with a handful of my clothes that he threw on the bed. He went back into the closet. Earrings, a handful of bracelets and a necklace were added to the pile of clothes. Shoes, panties, and a bra followed. He moved my things from one purse to another.

And looked over at me. "You have twenty minutes to get all of that shit on your body."

"My clothes aren't-"

"Figure of speech." He went to the kitchen and pulled out a pan, eggs, butter. "Get in the shower."

"You have to take a shower too."

He sniffed at himself. "Nope. I smell like you. I'm fine."

"I-" I shook my head and went into the bathroom.

Eggs, fruit, toast and a kiss waited for me when I was dressed and in the kitchen beside Cahir.

"Five minutes."

He was right. He did smell like me.

CHAPTER SIXTEEN

Cassidy

"How ridiculous should we be?"

We stood on a sidewalk on the East side of the City. On the street where all of the boutiques lived.

"We can go big box store first. Or we can just go full on dumb and go in one of these places and severely overpay for every single thing we buy."

"Or," I smiled when his hand slid into mine. "We can do this boutique thing and then we can go to Strawberry Fields and do some stuff there. And then we can drive to-"

"Stay local. Make a day of it. Got it." He kissed me. "Let's go embarrass ourselves."

"How?"

He didn't answer. He dragged me into a store. We wrapped ourselves in baby blankets and asked if we could lay on the mattresses in the cribs. We took pictures of them to see which ones looked better from "a consumer driven post-modernist point of view." We got on the floor and played with the blocks to see which of them could really hold our attention and make us want to play. I taught him how to cornrow using a dolls head. We both agreed he needed more practice.

"I kind of want a girl," he said after we apologized for holding a literary reading of the store's children's books.

"Really?"

"Yeah. Like I'll be happy either way but..."

"Is this like a princess thing?"

"Like I want a kid to spoil with nice things? No. I'm having a kid with you. Nice things were a given. Have you seen your apartment?"

"What about it?"

"How much did you pay for rugs? Just rugs?"

"I don't see how that's relevant."

We laughed.

"No. Just...I've seen you with your father. How you call him when you're lost even if I'm right there. Or when you wanna debate politics or understand how football works or go to a museum or...You know you called him once and said you just wanted to talk about yourself for a while?"

I laughed.

"Do you remember what he said?" Cahir smiled down at me. "He said, 'You're my favorite person in the world. Please do.'"

I wrapped my arms around Cahir.

"I want that. I want that kind of relationship."

"You'll have it," I said.

He kissed me. "We should test out the baby bottles. Let's go get some tequila and limes."

I laughed so loud it sounded like I was screaming.

∞

Cassidy

"So."

I looked up from my Korean barbecue. "Oh, God. We need to talk."

"This is talking." Cahir shook his head at me.

"This is a piece of beef that could ruin your shirt." I let it dangle from my chopsticks. "Are you sure this is the game you want to play?"

"You picked out this shirt."

"And I can ruin it. I have all the power here."

"It's not a bad talk. Release the meat."

"That's not what she said."

He laughed. At me. With me. It made me warm.

It was one in the morning. We both should have been asleep, but we were hungry. We burned dinner when we decided that putting our mouths and hands over each other, racing each other to orgasm, was more fun than cooking. We laid on the floor and laughed and eventually fell asleep. The growl of his stomach woke us. We tossed clothes at each other. Panties under the coffee table. His boxers bunched under a rug. A shoe in the kitchen, another close to the bed. My shirt almost all the way in the kitchen sink.

I drove us to the Korean barbecue restaurant. I made him laugh when he realized I knew almost all of the songs that played. He ran a finger down my neck and I forgot the words. I forgot where I was.

"What do we-" I cleared my throat and ignored the smile that crept across his face. "What do we need to talk about?"

"Lawyers."

"I have no specific feelings about them."

"I figured." His smile fell. "I'm talking about adoption lawyers, Cash."

"Oh."

"Yeah."

"We do need to talk."

"Yep."

I-I wasn't a stupid woman. I knew what I agreed to. I knew there would be a baby and I would be a mother and Cahir would be a father and we would be linked in more than one way for the rest of our life. I had baby things in my apartment and his. We built a crib. We went to another baby class. We knew how to handle the looks we got-the looks my flat stomach got. We talked about names. We decided to hyphenate the baby's last name and grinned about the pretentiousness of it all.

"There's going to be paperwork. It can't go through until Zion-When that happens-"

"Is that going to happen?"

He barely looked at me but that was enough. "Yeah. O'Shea hired a lawyer. There's going to be a meeting. At Beyond."

"When did you find out?" I was proud of myself. My voice stayed even.

"Today. The lawyer called me. Then O'Shea called me. There might have been something like an apology in there for getting to me after the lawyer."

I laughed. And was glad I remembered how when the rest of my body felt like it was racing towards something I didn't need.

"I-" He draped an arm over my chair and played with the curl behind my left ear. He always found that one curl no matter how I styled my hair. I left it down for him and thought that that was what love was-what compromise was. "I knew-I know I'm going to be a father. I know I'm going to have a child. I know I'm going to be its primary guardian. I know I don't want Zion to have access to my kid. I know we're doing this together. And I still sat in my office and just...didn't know what to do."

The racing stopped. It stopped so suddenly that I was dizzy. I turned to him. "I love you."

"I love you."

"An attorney."

"Yeah. An adoption attorney."

"Because we're doing this."

"Not just the classes." He pulled my curl just a little as he wound it around his fingers in a pattern I sometimes traced over his chest. I didn't know which of us taught the other.

"Not just the shopping."

"A little person that's going to need us."

"We need them. Right?"

He looked at me. "That's what I wanted to ask you. Do you need this? Babies are messy, expensive, disruptive. Your whole life, my whole life, they're going to change completely. Do you want your life to change?"

I nodded. "When should we go see the lawyer?"

∞

Cassidy

We saw the lawyer the next day. At Cahir's office. I didn't think about that. The logistics of it. Not until Cahir gave me his executive chair and leaned against it. Not until all of the paperwork was laid in front of us and the attorney smiled at us and said he was so glad, so grateful that he could help us build our family in such a sincere way that I had no choice but to believe him.

Then I looked around at the office that was maybe a little too familiar to me. I saw the place where I stood and asked Cahir why he left me. I saw the places where he made me call his name when there was no one to hear us but the darkness a few weeks later. I smiled up at him. He smiled back.

"Places carry memories, right?" And he kissed me and turned his attention back to the lawyer and the stacks and mountains of paperwork.

A small thing. Such a small thing. But everything inside of me was aflame. A gentle flame that told me it could be an inferno; we could be an inferno. We could bathe the world in a light that would make it so much more. And he was— Cahir's attention was on the attorney. As if he hadn't just changed everything for me in a way that was so quiet I almost didn't hear it.

I pushed the feelings down and tuned in to the attorney. I ignored the buzzing of my phone. A different buzz for each of my social media platforms. Another for customers. One for Delia.

Delia.

I would deal with that another day.

I read through the paperwork and realized there was a legal definition for motherhood. That was what hit me first. Words mean things. They carry responsibilities. I knew that. I did. But there were laws. The number of people that could sleep in a bedroom together. How fast that number dropped if their genders changed.

What had to be in the home, in my baby's bedroom, if I didn't want to be accused of neglect. The condition of their clothing. Their smell. Someone could call Child Protective Services if they were offended by the way my baby smelled. Would they find my herbs and flowers and oils offensive? Could celebrating my culture get my family torn from me?

Weight and feedings and visits and growth charts. Intelligence charts.

The attorney looked around the office. "I don't think those things will be too much of a problem for you guys."

The flame inside me turned darker. Almost white in its blinding power. Because he was right. Money. Money would make all the difference. Money would mean that no one would think to look at us. They would never think our child could be hurt or abused. Any visits we got would be a formality. Any opposition-quickly squashed. Because of something as common and degrading as money.

Cahir ran a hand across my shoulder, traced out the shell of my ear. I breathed. One deep breath after another.

"Thank you," I said.

"Yeah," he said. "You need a break?"

I nodded. The attorney walked out before we could ask him to.

Cahir sat on the corner of his desk and faced me.

"I've never seen motherhood boiled down this way." I let the corners of one stack of papers slide down my thumb. "I feel like-There's no emotion in this. I didn't expect there to be. This is the legal side of things. But still..."

"But still?"

"Motherhood boiled down to a list of duties that I don't even really have to uphold because I have a decent amount of money and my partner has an obscene amount."

He looked away.

"You can laugh."

He did. "I don't think it's obscene."

"No, no. Why would you?"

We laughed together.

"Is this all it is?" I gestured to the papers. "The size of a dresser or a bedroom? The quality of clothing? As long as there's stuff and no bruises or cuts? As long as they smell 'acceptable'?"

"You know it isn't. We know it isn't. That's what

matters. The paperwork is here for us to do this right, Cash. That's it. It's just here to make sure everyone knows. You decide what kind of mother you're going to be. We decide what kind of family we're going to be."

That was true. Did that truth make things better or worse?

CHAPTER SEVENTEEN

Cahir

O'Shea had to know that her voice carried. She was never one to try to be silent but she had to hear Cassidy and I climb the stairs. Nadia had to know she yelled.

"Fair?" Nadia's voice was closer to a shriek. "What's fair about breaking up a family?"

"It's fair because she has a choice," O'Shea said.

I didn't know if Cash made a conscious decision to let her feet fall heavier on the stairs, but I did.

"She can give up the baby. And keep her life. Or she can give up the baby and go to jail," O'Shea said. "That's it. She can have mercy and privacy or she can have the law. Guy's lawyer says prosecuting her would be so easy a civilian could try the case. Ten years. She'd get at least ten years. Maybe get parole in three to five."

"Y'all probably don't want to listen to too much more of that." Guy was at the top of the stairs. He leaned against them. Dressed for work. Wore that easy smile that I heard was always there. Even when a situation called for violence. Especially then. "Let me show you where Arnold is."

Arnold, the attorney that had specific instructions to hide what a shark he was around Cash. He did his job well. She smiled at him, thanked him, before he left my office.

Guy took us to Zion's office and I wanted to laugh. Laughter would be better than the thing that blocked air from moving past my throat, that made me feel like I didn't have enough of something without knowing what the something was. Arnold was there. And when the door to Zion's office closed Nadia and O'Shea's voices left us.

He shook our hands and sat next to me at the long conference table that dominated the long thin room that used to be Zion's. I helped her find the table. The chairs. We found the lamps in an antique store. She told me not to worry about how much things cost-her sugar daddy was footing the bill. I shrugged. A work expense was a work expense. And I was different. I was personal.

I breathed in a little too fast and coughed.

Cash looked over at me. "I know. I know. But I'm here."

Always. And she got it. She knew to put her hand in mine and scratch a place just above my wrist. It was so jarring; it was all I could focus on. I didn't even realize that the door was open and Zion walked in with her attorney.

Cash's thumb pressed into my palm. I let my world shrink to that one place. Her skin on mine was where I lived and everything I felt could float around me. I could pick them up, my emotions, touch them, examine them, and be safe from them.

Anger was there. Not that she'd betrayed me. But because my first child should have been with Cash in every way. In a perfect world there would be no adoption. There would be no moments of hesitation from Cash as she tried not to think about exactly what she agreed to and all the ways she chose to link herself to me forever.

There would have been the wonder of the first kick, the discomfort that came towards the end. There would have been food cravings and mood swings and my hands on her as I marveled at all of the ways her body changed.

That was gone. I would never be able to give Cash that because someone stole it from me.

Shock. Zion was pregnant. The hand that she rested over her stomach-my baby was there. Cash and I's baby was there.

Shock that it was Zion. After so much time I thought it would be different. I thought everything that made me who I was would chip and fall away until I crumbled all at once.

I thought I would rub my fingers over those scars and remember that night. I thought I would feel the blood slither between my fingers and the shards of glass that clung to me as reminders that it was all real. I hadn't dreamed it.

Instead there was detachment. Zion was beautiful. I recognized it the way I recognized the beauty in art that would never hang in my home. I saw luxury. I saw elegance.

And I saw the way O'Shea looked at Zion.

I recognized that I'd never loved Zion. I wanted her. Clung to her. Created a world with her. But there was never real love. If there were my expression would be identical to O'Shea's. Close to Nadia's.

They sat further down the table. Directly across from Zion. And wasn't that telling. That Zion didn't choose to sit across from me. She arranged herself in the chair that she knew O'Shea would take. And they...I'd never seen a bird struggle to fly, to be free, to find home again, but I imagined it was what the two of them looked like.

They threw words across the table at each other while I stayed in the space Cash made for me. O'Shea put her wrists on the table and I remembered that she'd cut them with a boxcutter right after she married Guy. Maybe because of Guy.

Another person that bled for love.

Huh.

But they were different. The way he touched her. The way her body angled towards his. The way she seemed to see Zion but be focused completely on him. The way he was obviously focused solely on her.

There was something between them that was so awful at one point that she cut her wrists and yet there they were in that moment. Almost one single being.

Wonder was the next emotion I found. It showed me another side to the fear. It showed me the worry I didn't know I was carrying that Cash would always pull away from me for just a little while and we would both know it was because of the elevator. An incident that lasted a handful of minutes that affected us for months after. I thought it would drag behind us forever. Maybe it would. And maybe we could get to what O'Shea and Guy had. Together. With the truth of what they'd both done to each other right there, literally, on the table.

I didn't need to be there. I didn't have to sign anything. I didn't have to say anything. What would I say? "Hey, it's cool. I found the love of my life and we're going to raise the kid I didn't want with you but can't wait to have with her."

O'Shea would be upset that she didn't have a monopoly on cruelty.

Cash made a fist on the table. I laid a hand over it. None of it mattered. It wasn't about us. O'Shea and Zion would accuse each other of things in low tones. Eventually Zion would have to do what she came to Beyond to do.

I held Cash's hand in mine and waited. Let my mind wander. I found solutions to two different issues I had with apps my company was developing. I decided where I would take Cash on our next vacation. I did the math to try and guess how much college would cost by the time the baby was ready to go. I turned a little green.

Cash shook me. I came out of my quiet place to hear Zion say, "Did you bring the paperwork?"

∞

Cassidy

I looked up photos of Zion before the meeting. I...It would have been stupid not to. I sat on my bed while Cahir was in the shower and smiled when I heard him sing. Then I looked down at my phone. At the search bar and the blinking cursor. My fingers slipped across the keyboard. I almost dropped my phone before I finished typing in her name. Me-the woman who could type without looking down at her phone on any other day.

And there she was. With him. Without him. She was stunning.

And I was okay.

I dropped my phone and took in a deep breath when I realized that. I was okay. And she was just the woman that got to hold my baby before I did.

I wrapped my legs, then my arms, then my mouth around Cahir when he got out of the shower and laughed when he stepped back into the shower with me.

The meeting was-Well, it became pretty obvious, pretty quickly that we were absolutely unnecessary. It wasn't about the baby. It was about O'Shea and Zion and one last knock down drag out battle before O'Shea banished her forever.

Or that was what I would have said if I didn't feel the energy in that room. I'd never seen two people that wanted to be close, to touch, so badly. Anger born out of hurt and disappointment and a longing that it could all be forgiven and forgotten.

I found myself feeling sorry for each of them until she talked about Cahir as if he were a thing, just a piece of her life, the way her closet or her chauffeur were. It all belonged to her so it should all fall in line.

And the baby. A girl. Olivia, they called her. I loved that name. I grew up with re-runs of the Cosby show. Too young to understand most of what I saw but I remembered that there was a girl like me that showed up. One that had things to say and think and could make you laugh without trying. I used to hope that one day I could be that bright. I wanted to light up a room the way Olivia did.

I glanced at Cahir but his eyes were on our hands. Was he here for any of it? Was I?

Then Zion asked for the paperwork and it was real. A family.

Olivia.

CHAPTER EIGHTEEN

Cassidy

I didn't stay to watch Zion sign the papers. Cahir's pulse was normal. He made eye contact. His leg didn't shake quite so much. I went back to work. Then I came back to him when it was all over.

Except it wasn't really over. Zion's lawyer gave us pictures from the ultrasound. They were supposed to be part of her last attempt to get Cahir back. Her lawyer slid them to Cahir before he left.

He waited for me. I loved him for that. He waited until our days were over and we were curled up on my couch to hand me the envelope. I put my wine down. The tears started before I saw all of the first photo.

"Olivia." I hid my face in his neck. "Did you hear that? That she'd named the baby Olivia."

"No." His voice was as bogged down with emotion as mine was. "I didn't."

"Gran says even a broken clock is right twice a day."

He laughed. "So you like that name."

"I think it's perfect." I wiped his tears. His thumb caught mine. "Is that weird?"

"A good name is a good name."

We sat with the pictures spread on the couch between us. Spread wide but not so much that my hand couldn't find his. That his fingers couldn't play in my hair.

"So…Olivia?"

I nodded. "Olivia."

I floated for days. Days. I carried the pictures in my purse. The ones that Cahir didn't stash in his car, office, and apartment.

Reality was there while I floated. I had clients to deal with. Delia. I could see her from where we sat at her desk in her loft office. She didn't know that. There was no way she would have stood and sat, looked over at us in Zion's office, looked at Zion, picked up her phone and put it down if she knew we could see her.

I could see the way she watched me.

When had O'Shea told her what Cahir was to me? When did Delia find out that I was going to be a mother? She wasn't different when we worked together. But that was easy. We didn't really see each other. She was busy with her online boutique. I was busy with the styling side and I was good enough at my job that I didn't need any real input from her.

But I knew when I walked into the office and turned on my tablet that she would find me before my first client arrived. She saw the cowboy boots Cahir found for me when he went on a business trip and I wanted to smile. We had more in common than she thought. Shoes changed how I dealt with a person too.

I sat on the sofa surrounded by the clothes she sold and the racks I used to dress clients. By the props I used when I took photos of them for their social media and waited.

She sat down beside me. "Cassidy, can we talk?"

"Sure." Best to address it head on. "How are you doing? With everything? I know the last few days have been tough for you guys."

Bless her. Her facial expression didn't change. Still. Calm. Delia had grown so much since her first day as a stylist. "It has been difficult. Some of the things I've learned have made it a little more difficult."

Oh.

Well.

"Your relationship with Cahir."

My father taught me that to save your ground, to gain a little more, become a parrot. Repeat it all until people stop wasting your time and get to the point. "Cahir and I?"

"You're having a relationship with a client."

That didn't take long. "Okay."

"Without telling me."

"Why would I do that?"

"Excuse me?"

And there she was. Good. My client would arrive soon. "It's not interfering with the quality of my work. Obviously or you wouldn't have had to be told about it. It hasn't affected his status as a client or my ability to bring in or maintain my clients. And there's noting in the employee conduct paperwork that I signed that forbids or discourages it."

I checked. Based on Delia's facial expression, she hadn't.

"I would have liked to know," she said. "It's not fun hearing things about my business second-hand."

"What did you hear about your business?"

"I-"

Fishing. I hated that. "I could have told you. Sure. But something, something, told me not to."

She angled her body away from me. Smoothed down her skirt.

"In the beginning, it was because I wasn't about it. He's an amazing man. Of course I was attracted to him. Then I got to know him. What kind of business did I have messing with a man with so much going on in his life, a man that was admittedly trying to get over his feelings for another woman." I smoothed a hand down my skirt and adjusted an earring that didn't need to be adjusted. So Delia wouldn't feel alone. "Then I got to know him. He showed up- doesn't matter. I got to know him. I liked him. I wanted to be his friend. I didn't have to tell you who my friends were."

I shrugged. She stared.

"Then it was so new I couldn't believe it was real and any little thing would have ruined it." God, those early days. That first trip to the farmer's market. That late night in that dark bar. "And I just didn't want to share it. I wanted to keep the beautiful thing to myself. The reason why I haven't told you now? Why I'm not talking about it? I'm not apologizing. I'm not telling you that I've found someone to love and then apologizing for who it is. That's not something I have to do and even if it was, it ain't something I'm going to do."

Whoa. Too much Baltimore. I usually had more control over how much of home showed up in my voice.

"Okay," Delia said.

She went up to her desk.

I went back to work. And thanked the ancestors I wasn't stupid enough to think the conversation was over.

∞

Cassidy

"It'll be easier for you if you tell me on your own." Cahir laid his napkin on my dinner table and leaned back in his chair. He was shirtless. That wasn't fair. "If I have to fuck it out of you, you won't realize you enjoyed it until the next day. Maybe the day after."

Wildly unfair. I put my napkin on the chair and ran a finger around the rim of my wine glass. Weighed my options and sighed. I didn't want to cry during sex. Not that kind of crying at least. "Delia's going to fire me."

"What?" He grabbed my hand and moved my wine away. "Why?"

"I need that."

"I'm stretching you across that bed either way. No, you don't."

"She doesn't like that I'm with her sister's ex boyfriend."

"Childish."

I shrugged. "She's young."

"You're good at your job."

"You'd think that would count for something."

"Do you need to work for Delia?"

"It's better than working for anyone else. And I need to work."

"What?"

"It's better than-"

"No, the second part." There was a crease between his eyebrows.

"I need to work."

"You need to work? Why?"

I waved an arm. "All of this doesn't pay for itself. That closet doesn't just replenish itself automatically."

"Money? You're upset about this job situation because of money?"

"Why is this so confusing for you?"

"Because-Cash." His fingers tightened over mine. He was close enough for me to smell the wine on his breath. To want to kiss him and taste the wine again in a different way. "You're my best friend and the mother of my child. Money isn't an issue for you anymore."

"What?"

"That's my line."

I tried to smile and failed. I could see how badly I failed by the way his face shifted, he bit his lip, and looked away.

"Cash," he said when his shoulders stopped shaking. "You're family. Before Olivia you were family. You're good."

"I'm good."

"You're an investor in all of the software I develop. I started a trust for you when I started one for Olivia. You're very good."

"What in the hell?"

"You know...this was kind of the reaction I thought I would get."

"So you shoveled heinous amounts of money-"

"You sound like the beginning of Law and Order: SVU." He laughed. "And we're having an Olivia. That's so corny it's funny."

"Is it?"

"Cash, it's money. I have it. I want to share it with the two most important women in my life. What's the problem?"

That he thought to take care of me that way. That it wasn't something friends did for each other. That it tied us together in ways I told him I couldn't consider. That I loved him for doing it and couldn't remember why I said I wasn't ready to be with him.

I sighed. "Take me to bed."

CHAPTER NINETEEN

Cassidy

It was there in the way she didn't say good morning to me after I said it to her. It was there in the way she stayed upstairs at her desk and didn't come down to interact with her favorite clients. It was there in the way Nadia and O'Shea gave me sympathetic looks and a whole lot of silence when they went up the stairs.

Okay. I breathed through it. Meditated when I entered and left the office. Burned herbs and left crystals to rebalance the energy after she left. I put on music that settled my soul. And I smiled.

No one was allowed to take away my smile.

I brought in more clients. I was proud of that. I went out to bars and restaurants and the farmer's market and events with and without Cahir and handed out my business cards. So many business cards that reaching for them and re-ordering them felt like second nature. The women and men came to me. The racks that surrounded me bulged with clothes. Local stores called me-they called me.

They set up appointments for me to see them. I didn't have to beg for their attention or for them to take me seriously.

And I had offers. To manage social media accounts. To dress celebrities. They didn't want Beyond or Delia. They wanted me.

I couldn't remember the last time I'd felt so strong, so capable. I couldn't remember the last time I'd jumped out of bed ready to go to work. I couldn't remember the last time I felt so valuable and respected in the workplace.

But that was what working for someone that didn't want to limit you was like. Room. Expansion. Trust in a different form. Confidence that you would be heard.

So I smiled at Delia. I said good morning and good night and didn't care if she responded. Until one day.

She came in not with the coffee that she grabbed every morning with Colton but with something O'Shea must have made. Comfort. Strength. Or it was supposed to be. Support made her smile. She didn't smile when she stomped up to her office.

She wasn't quiet when she scheduled meetings.

I took another deep breath and smiled. To myself. For myself. Everything was going to be okay.

It took her three hours to come back down the stairs. I was ready. I'd picked a place to have a drink with Junie and Cahir. I told Cahir what I thought would happen. He asked how disrespectful I felt and if the Lonely Third was empty. I didn't laugh aloud. I ran around the office manically looking for a way to wipe away the tears rolling down my face. I packed up my files.

I was mostly done with packing up my files when Delia walked down the stairs.

"I need your resignation."

I put my smile away. Delia didn't need it. I could see it

in the way her hands shook and she hesitated at the bottom of the stairs.

I took a moment to check in with myself. Gran taught me that. In all situations, but especially high conflict situations, check in with yourself before you speak. Find your emotions. Identify them. Find their source. Make peace with them before you speak.

No anger. No fear. No worry. Because Cahir said I didn't have to worry. Because even if I didn't admit it to him or admit it to myself, I believed him. And I was with him. He was mine again. I was his. I knew we'd never have another elevator situation again. He would never hide from me again. I didn't have a reason to hide from him.

I wanted to go to him. I wanted to meet him on the Lonely Third or lock the door to his office. I didn't know how I would tell him. But I wanted him close.

I put more files in my container. "Are you sure?"

"You said the conflict of interest wouldn't stop. That you're adopting my niece. Yeah. I'm sure."

Poor Delia. She would hate that that was the first thought to enter my mind. But there was so much hurt there. I could do it on my own. And her business would survive without me. She'd grown so much. But why should we break up a good thing?

"Forty percent increase in revenue. Think, Delia. Forty percent. You want to let that go for a woman that betrayed you and isn't sorry about it? A woman that violated Ca-"

"You don't know her, so don't speak about her."

"You know me." I put dirty glasses in the small dishwasher by the wine fridge. "And you know better."

I picked up the box with my files. I should have gotten something with wheels. "If I leave, my clients come with me. You know that. So I won't resign yet. But I will take a few days off. Think, Delia. Think. We're doing something amazing here. I'm giving you the room you need to expand this business into something breathtaking." I shook my hair out of my face. "And I didn't do anything wrong. It's not me you want to punish."

But she would do it anyway. I saw it in the way her stance adjusted. Shoulders a bit higher. Little hands balled into fists. Pretty little mouth ready to snarl.

"No." I shook my head. "You're hurting. I understand that. And when you realize it too, we're going to go back to being friends and working together. Unless you say something else. Something you don't mean and don't believe because you just want to hurt me. I'm leaving."

I had to grip my box of files tighter but the truth always made it easier for me to hold things otherwise too heavy for me.

I made it to the door and realized there was more. Just a little bit more. "I trust you. I trust you to make the right decision. Don't let me down, okay? You're one of the only people that never has."

∞

Cahir

She said it was okay. She came when I told her to. She nudged and maneuvered until her body was as close to mine as it could be when we laid beside each other at night. She still danced when we cooked and in the car. She smiled. And she sat with her client files around her on the floor.

She organized and reorganized them. She pasted on a smile when she told them that she had to take a few unexpected days out of the office but of course she would be back. She took clothes to the ones that had events. Things she had to go to different boutiques and stores to get because she couldn't go back to Beyond. And she checked her phone again and again. She wouldn't tell me why but I knew. Everything would change if she got just one text from Delia.

I woke up early that Sunday. Before the sun and walked to the farmer's market. I loved that it was close enough for me to do that. Loved that the only reason why we drove was because we knew we'd do a bit too much.

"Yeah. I'll take all of this. Can you be at my house in thirty minutes?"

Maybe Cash's favorite florist would have said no if I hadn't put an envelope in her hand.

She smiled. "I can be there in fifteen. Wanna ride with me?"

I did. And left her in the parking garage while I ran into the apartment. Cash was in my bed where I left her. She barely woke up when I slid one of my t-shirts over her naked body. She smiled when I kissed her and early morning breath washed over my face.

God, I-

I helped the florist bring bucket after bucket of flowers into the house. She smiled and closed the door softly behind her. I found the pruning shears Cash insisted I needed and rolled my shoulders.

"Okay. I can do this."

The sun had just reached across the bed to warm her face when Cash turned and did what I knew she would. Wipe a hand across her eyes. Open them a bit. She sat up. And the flowers I'd spread across the bed and on my pillow moved to accommodate her.

I leaned against the wall and watched her take it in then decided I wanted to take it in with her.

In the time while I waited for her to wake up, I'd filled every vase, wine glass, cup, rocks glass, champagne flute and bucket I could find with the flowers I bought her. They crowded in every open space they could find, every flat surface. An explosion of color and scent and texture.

"Wanna go to the farmer's market?"

She wiped the tears from her face and turned to me. "Come here."

She was on her knees. They sank into the mattress just a bit. Her hands cradled my face. My hands reached for hers. She leaned into my touch. The sun cradled us both. And she was back. For the first time since she came home from Beyond with that box too full and too heavy for her to carry, she was with me.

"How do you always know?"

"Because you show me. You're smart like that." I kissed her while she laughed.

The laughter stopped. I spread her legs before I put my mouth on her and smelled the heavy, softness of lavender. I lapped at her, swallowed her, and there was the dusky, lightness of tuberose. The luxury and decadence of dahlias when her hands reached for the headboard and her back arched. Baby's breath tickled my sides when I locked my arms around her thighs and held her down. It was called common lilac but I didn't think there was anything common about the smell of it and her as she shook against my mouth.

Gardenia when I kissed my way up her body. And there-a flower known only as pink when I slid inside her. As her body got slick with sweat it mingled with the smell of peony and freesia. When her legs and arms locked around me-sweet pea and mock oranges.

When we came together, I only smelled us.

CHAPTER TWENTY

Cahir

We made it to the farmer's market because I ignored her. The way she smiled at me. Giggled up at me. Pouted when I didn't join her in the shower. When she got out of that shower and water cascaded down her body. I gave her a towel and ran. Her laughter, throaty and aware, chased after me.

She held my hand when she thanked the florist. When she stepped into the sun and turned those brown eyes to me-When would she stop being such a miracle?

"Tell me," I said.

"I-" She sighed. "All of it?"

"Even the parts that might bother me a little."

"They might bother you a lot."

"Tell me."

She kissed me and gripped my hand a little tighter. "I've made so many decisions in the past few months. Well, no-I've made one decision and everything else has been a consequence of that."

I thought I knew where the conversation was going and didn't know how I felt.

"The baby. I decided to be a mother and it felt like my life kind of fell apart as a response?"

She didn't look at me. That was good. I needed her to finish.

"The attorney. The paperwork. The showdown with Zion that we shouldn't have fucking been at."

I laughed. "True."

"Losing my job. I decide to become a mother and I lose my job. What the fuck is that? I mean-I know it's a thing that happens to women. I do. On an intellectual level. But I still can't believe it happened to me. Especially since I work for a woman."

"Is it that you decided to become a parent or who you chose to parent? Who you chose to parent with?"

"I wouldn't do this with anyone else."

Everything in me froze for a second. My next breath felt new.

"It's not supposed to be like this. I'm not supposed to-" She shrugged. "I'm not supposed to lose. Not now."

No. She wasn't. And it must have felt like she had been from the moment she told me she loved me and found out seconds later that my ex was pregnant. What had I lost?

I rubbed a hand on the back of my neck.

"What?"

"Nothing. It's selfish if you tell me something and then I start talking about myself. It's…high school."

She threw back her head and laughed. "I love you. I love you so much. Tell me."

"I don't know how to help you. That's-Even if I can't solve your problems-"

"-you want to solve my problems."

I shrugged. "And I can't. I can't take this away from you

and make it better. I can't hand you your job back. I can't make it easier with the baby, everything. That's a struggle for me. How can I help?"

"This helps." She wrapped her arms around me. "That you want to help. That you ask. That you listen."

"Can't be that easy."

"Sometimes."

ᗡᗡ

Cassidy

Cahir's money wasn't the issue. Making money in general wasn't the issue. I still had clients. They crowded into my apartment and cooed over my plants. At how *grounded* everything was. They threw around their money in Gran's shop. So much that she came to demand why we hadn't done this sooner and to ask if I wanted the empty apartment across the hall from me.

"It would be a nice studio space for you," Gran said.

It would. And it felt good. Welcoming. North facing windows and original hardwood floors. I could see it.

And didn't want it.

I wanted Beyond. I wanted whispered jokes with Junie and conspiratorial winks with O'Shea as she swapped out the wines Delia bought for her own "better" picks. I wanted the space. I wanted the room. I wanted less responsibility.

A baby and potentially a new business? In the world of "women can do it all," I knew I couldn't do that. Even if I could, why would I want to? The drive to push, to have more, to do more, to be more, seemed at war with everything that I was.

I wanted expansion. I wanted adventure. I wanted to be intentional. I wanted to be creative. I wanted to do less. I wanted to do it all for me. Not to prove that I made it. I wanted lazy mornings and early nights because I said so.

I didn't want the grind, and I was proud of it.

I tossed and turned at night. Pulled Cahir from his sleep and touched him until he understood that I needed him to help my mind rest. It would work for a while. A few hours. Then the weight would return.

What did you do when you didn't want it all?

∞

Cahir

"I want a baby," I said at the dinner table.

My parents laughed.

"And what will you do with it if we find one for you?" My father leaned back in his chair.

"Play with it."

Wasn't that obvious? It was obvious to my five year old self and my parents were so much smarter than me. They knew everything. Except how to stop arguing.

"And when it cries? When it makes a mess in its pants? When it wants to be fed? When it wants things and you don't know what it wants and you think you'll pull your hair out before you find a way to make the noise stop?" My father cut into his steak as if he hadn't turned my world upside down.

"They do that?"

"Boy-o. They do that and more." He leaned across the table towards me. That wasn't normal-that I ate dinner with my parents and didn't have to wear a suit. All my friends had to dress up for dinner with their parents. But they didn't do it every night like we did. They didn't just eat at the kitchen table like we did. They didn't get to help cook like I did. Or wash dishes. Because dinner was fancy. Fancy dinners sounded boring. "Babies, children, a family. That's a big decision, Cahir. The only decision you can't take back once you make it."

"Like a puppy." I nodded.

They laughed.

"But different. Because the puppy will become a dog but it will always be what you trained it to be. Children-" He sighed. "A risk. You hope, and you want, and you wish for them. But they'll be who they'll be and you must do your best and hope for the best. You teach them but you're never sure they'll learn."

I mulled it over as my mother cut my steak and gave a pointed look to my vegetables. I put my chin in my hands. I was going to eat them. I helped make them, didn't I?

I thought a baby would be fun. Something to play with and put away when my friends came to visit or I got a new book or Dad let me help him pull things apart in the garage. I liked that best of all. To see how things worked. To find new ways to use old things.

But a decision I couldn't take back? What if I got it and it didn't stop crying? And-oh! It would stop being a baby one day. What if, no matter what I did, it became a person I didn't like? What if it didn't want to play? Or it always wanted to play and didn't leave me alone? What if it didn't like me? What if Mom and Dad liked it better than me? Would they send me back?

I ate dinner in silence. My parents talked around me and about me but left me to my thoughts.

"No baby," I said when my plate was clear. "A puppy?"

They laughed.

My father's hand was comforting, familiar, when it ruffled my hair. "Maybe, son."

They never got me the puppy. I never asked again about a baby.

I was happy.

Cahir

She wasn't better. At all.

I worried over that as I smiled at ultrasound pictures and our joint efforts to baby proof our apartments. Odd to hold two things in my head like that at once.

I woke her early one morning with the sound of the zippers on her suitcase. "Let's go."

She sat straight up. She'd been awake for hours. Her usual morning routine gone. She would lay there and stare at the ceiling. Never at me. Never a smile. A curl of her toes. A stretch. "Where are we going?"

"Your bag is packed."

She shrugged. "Okay. Let me get dressed."

"Your clothes are in the bathroom," I said.

And here's all the trust between us.

I shook my head. No time for that. Or too much. A lifetime to just...have her. To stop in my tracks because she let me handle it without question.

She reclined against me after we got settled on the jet. "What are we doing?"

Not where are we going. Not where are you taking me. Not when will I be home. Not Cahir, I have to work. Just a soft body against mine and a voice as familiar as my own. Softer than her body.

"We're leaving it alone for a little while."

"What?" She burrowed deeper into my side.

"That thing that's keeping you up all night. That shit you can't control no matter how much you worry about it."

"What?"

"You really are turning into me." I smiled when she laughed. Kissed the top of her head. "The job. The baby. It's all going to happen how it happens. No matter how much sleep you lose over it. So we're gonna stop fucking our way through it and relocate for a little while."

She grinned. The one that told me my eyes would probably cross and I'd start questioning my own existence.

She straddled me. "We really have to stop fucking our way through it?"

I helped her take her pants off. I didn't give her panties. So wet. "Maybe not."

Cash did this thing with her hips when she was on top of me- a rock and a bounce. Her hair got as wild as she did. Her voice got deeper, every sound and syllable a little longer. Her hands got greedy. So did her mouth. When she was done with me it felt like she was everywhere and determined to take me with her.

I was lucky that I wanted to go.

I took her to the mountains. The first snow was on the ground. Enough to make you catch your breath. Not enough to bring out the skiers and snowboarders. It felt like we were alone in a world all our own.

On the first day, we hiked. My idea. She complained until we reached a clearing that gave us a view into the valley below us.

She grabbed my hand. Squeezed it. "You remind me to believe in things."

I learned there were words better than "I love you".

Another day we went shopping. Or we shopped together. I tried to pick out clothes for myself. She laughed at my choices. I picked out clothes for her. The things she did to me in the changing room would have gotten us arrested if she hadn't stuffed her panties in my mouth.

"Foresight." She kissed me. Broad sweeps of her tongue

so I could familiarize myself with the way I tasted. "That's what they call it."

"Hustle," I said and had her on her back in the hotel room in under half an hour.

"Oh, I like this," she said, breath heavy. Chest rising and falling in ways that would have made me nervous any other time. "I like your hustle."

I took my tongue off her clit. "Tell me what else you like."

She did. Until she was screaming the words. Until she couldn't find words at all.

We went to dinner in a place that we had no business at. Not because I couldn't afford it, or because we didn't dress for it. Cash was gorgeous. Her dress was long. Almost the exact color of her skin. The slit up the front of that dress was the reason I decided we could recreate Miami and slid under the table. I grinned when she let me spread her legs so wide, so fast, the slit in dress grew a few inches. I laughed into her when her legs shook around my head. Fell silent when food was brought to our table. It smelled good. I didn't want them to kick us out before I could enjoy it.

"This is good," I said to a slumped over Cash. "Do you think it's because it tastes a little like you? Try it."

She rolled her eyes at me.

I worked while she slept. Checked on Olivia's accounts, hers, while her hand snaked up my leg. Seductive even when she was asleep, her favorite satin cap slipping back on her head.

"I love you," I said into the dark sure she wouldn't respond.

"I love you too," she said.

Because she was always there. Even when I didn't know I needed her to be.

CHAPTER TWENTY-ONE

Cassidy

He reminded me to believe in things. He reminded me to believe in myself and my power to make everything right for me. He reminded me that I wasn't alone.

He dragged me all over that mountain. And waited. So I gave him what he wanted.

I talked.

And talked. And talked. And talked.

He didn't tell me I was wrong. He didn't lay judgment over me. That was good. My guilt was heavy enough. He just...listened.

And I felt it fall away. I felt it-it didn't leave. But it was different. Something small enough to hold in my hands. Not something that laid heavy over my shoulders, a cumbersome burden that I could never find the right way to carry.

I woke up on, maybe, our fifth day in the mountains and stretched, smiled, reached for him.

He kissed me. "We can go home whenever you want."

"Or we could stay a little longer."

His weight pressed me deeper into the bed. I welcomed it-that grounding. "We could stay a little longer."

My body rose as the sun did. Higher and higher until finally he whispered in my ear that it was okay. I could give it to him. All of it. Then everything went dark.

I came back into myself with a laugh. "Let's go home."

We did. He showed me how sturdy the walls of the jet were. How soundproof the bedroom on that sleek little plane was. And he waved hello to Gran as if his fingers didn't smell like me.

Exertion wasn't the reason I panted as we climbed the stairs.

"Okay."

Against my door. It hurt my back and my hips. I threw my head back, once, just a little too hard. But that was just fine. He always made the pain worth it.

The indents he left in my ass. The burn of pulled hair. The tightness, the panic, that came with his hand around my neck. The burn of thighs spread wider and wider than they ever had been before.

Oh, he was worth it. Every moment. Every second. Every whimper I pushed into his mouth and every time my fingers curled and clawed into him, an attempt to find a safe space. Something to hold onto.

We showered together after we tumbled into my apartment. Laughed and kissed and he laughed when I moaned every time he found another place that was sore and tired.

He made dinner while I unpacked, and we yelled at each other across the apartment over the sounds of cooking and a New Orleans DJ's mix that he knew I would love.

I laughed when he twerked. He bit his lip when I did.

That was different. I was different. So different from

that girl that snuck into the club and met a man and loved him through the night and all the storms we made.

He was plating dinner. Crispy polenta and chicken thighs cooked under a weight so the skin would crunch like a chip. Brussel sprouts with almost as much bacon as Brussels. I opened wine.

His phone rang.

He didn't turn. Just saw my face and scooped more Brussel sprouts onto my plate. I made another face and he gave me more polenta.

His phone rang again.

And I heard mine ringing. Muffled by all the shit in my purse.

We both froze.

His phone was there on the counter. He didn't reach for it so I did.

So…It's happening.

O'Shea's text would have made me laugh at any other time. But…

"We should put some shoes on, huh?" Cahir slid our dinner into the oven.

There was humor in that too. I would have thrown it into the trash. What was a little more waste?

More than shoes. I had to dress. The sheer bra and panties, the satin robe. Not really hospital appropriate. We stood in the closet together and pulled things off hangers and out of drawers. When we were finished, we looked at each other.

It didn't look like we were going to the hospital. We could have been college students-grad students- on the way to grab coffee after a long night of drinking.

He helped me into my jacket. He grabbed his keys. There was the key to his car. To my home. To his home. His office. His world on one ring. He'd take his whole world with him to the hospital. And that rose quartz. A real piece of me in the room with him.

That was good. That was fine. Everything was fine.

"I'm an idiot for asking this." The timbre of his voice matched my mood. "You can say you aren't sure. That you aren't ready."

"The paperwork-"

"C'mon, Cash."

He was right. Paperwork could be shredded. But placing my hand in the one he offered to me. That was binding. Of all the things we did to prepare, that simple gesture would be the most real.

My hand rose over his. Not even an inch separated it. It shook. And my eyes met his.

ALSO BY JIMI GAILLARD-JEFFERSON

The New Money Girls

The New Money Girls

Zion, Nadia, Delia, and O'Shea have lives, dreams, and rich men who love them — but sex and money aren't always everything! Four friends will become a sisterhood in this sizzling page-turner.

Never Too Much

Sex and money aren't everything but that doesn't mean Zion, Nadia, Delia, and O'Shea can't have both. It doesn't mean they can't have it all. But can they be satisfied with having all of their dreams come true? Is happily ever enough?

Talk that Talk

Delia, O'Shea, and Nadia find out what happens to women bold enough to have it all and face consequences that will change them, and their sisterhood, forever.

Going to Hell

They were friends that became sisters and business partners. To keep love, ambition, their business, and their lifestyle, they'll have to become so much more.

Control

In the final book of the New Money Girls series, O'Shea, Nadia, and Delia will be tested in ways they never imagined. It's a good thing they have each other...

Guy

He saw her and knew. O'Shea saw him and resisted. He's never backed down from a fight- especially when his heart's on the line.

A FREE Standalone Novel.

The New Money Girls Complete Box Set

All five novels in the New Money Girls series in one place!

Tony and LeAndra

Belong to Me

Will king pin Tony quit the game for love? Will wealthy LeAndra give up her world to become a part of his? When their worlds collide sparks fly but so do tempers.

Conquer with Me

There's blood on her hands and at his feet. Can Tony and LeAndra rebuild their lives and the love they once shared?

Rule with Me

Can two lost souls find their way back to love and live life the way they'd planned: happily together?

Tony and LeAndra: The Complete Series Box Set

All three novels in the Tony and LeAndra series in one place!

Cassidy and Cahir

Better as Friends

He's strictly off limits. His ex ruined his life. Before he can move on I have to be sure his past is truly behind him.

Better than Your Ex

She lost him. She thinks it's over. She doesn't know that he's coming for her, that she's the love of his life.

Better as Lovers

He agreed to give her time. She agreed to stay by his side. Can the couple who had a bright future ahead of them, find their way past the obstacles and build a better future together or is it too late?

Friends to Lovers: The Complete Cassidy and Cahir Series

All three novels in the Cassidy and Cahir series in one place!

CPSIA information can be obtained
at www.ICGtesting.com
Printed in the USA
LVHW092038061120
670968LV00007B/1135